Keep up to d
and speci
joining his mail list at https://
bit.ly/3CILHI6. When you sign-up,
you'll get *Polderbeest* as a FREE gift.

SHADES &
SHADOWS

CATOCTIN TALL TALES & SHORT STORIES

by
J. R. Rada

AIM
PUBLISHING

SHADES & SHADOWS: CATOCTIN TALL TALES & SHORT STORIES

Published by AIM Publishing, a division of AIM Publishing Group.
Gettysburg, Pennsylvania.

ISBN: 978-1-7352890-9-0

The Anger of Innocence, Cast from the Gods, Old Kiln Road, Fire, Fire, and Set in Stone were published originally as serial stories in The Catoctin Banner under the name James Rada Jr.

CONTENTS

FOREWORD

Shades & Shadows is a project that grew out of an opportunity and inspiration.

Three years ago, in late 2019, I convinced the publisher of the *Catoctin Banner*, Deb Spalding, to let me write a serial story to help boost content for the newspaper's arts and entertainment page. I had seen this was popular in newspapers in the early 20th century from research I did for my history articles, and I wanted to see if I could revive it locally.

In the old newspapers, a new chapter in a serial story was

published weekly. Since the *Catoctin Banner* is a monthly publication, my stories would be published once a month over six to eight consecutive months.

Another big difference between my serials and those in old newspapers would be that my stories would be connected to the community within the newspaper's circulation area. The strength of a small newspaper like the *Catoctin Banner* is that it contains news and information for the local area that people aren't likely to read in larger newspapers. I thought my stories should also play to this strength.

I was delighted when Deb agreed to publish the serial, but then I had to come up with a story. I got to work and wrote "The Anger of Innocence." It is set primarily in Rocky Ridge, Maryland, and centers on the millions of birds that settled in the town for weeks in the early 1970s and the damage they caused. This was a real event, by the way.

Although I had originally only planned to write the one story as "The Anger of Innocence" neared completion, Deb asked me what was next. I was more than happy to come up with a new story because by that point, I had gotten hooked on writing serials.

So I wrote another one and another. I switched up genres sometimes to be able to offer something for everyone. I got encouraging feedback when I met locals who had read the stories, which encouraged me to keep writing them.

I started coming up with story ideas and outlining them. A couple are long enough that I might actually turn them into novels. Others might not make the cut, depending on what other ideas I come up with.

Fast forward three years, and I realize I have a nice collection of serials with more on the way. As I was planning out future books I would publish, the thought hit me that I could collect the serials into a collection. I had done it successfully with non-fiction articles I have written.

I liked the idea, but it took me a while to settle on a way to present it. The easiest way would have been to collect the serials that had been published in the newspaper and publish them as a multi-genre collection.

The more I thought about it, though, the more I thought it wouldn't fly. Readers tend to like certain genres. My horror fans probably wouldn't appreciate my romance serials and vice versa.

As I looked at the material I had and what I had planned, I decided to create three different volumes of *Catoctin Tales & Short Stories*. Each volume will focus on a specific genre. Hence, you have in your hands *Shades & Shadows*: *Catoctin Tall Tales & Short Stories*. The other two that will eventually come out are The Romance Collection and The Thriller Collection.

This doesn't mean that I'm done with horror serials. It just means that I would need to write another set to come out with another title. Meanwhile, I am working on the other two collections.

So, I hope you enjoy this collection of horror stories. Let me know what you think.

J. R. Rada
February 19, 2023

THE ANGER OF INNOCENCE

CHAPTER 1: TAKING FLIGHT

The blackbird fell out of the sky, diving so close to Christine Weber's head that the blonde thirteen-year-old had to duck to keep the bird from tangling in her hair. She flapped her arms over her head trying to drive it off. When it didn't land in her hair or claw at her, Christine straightened up and looked around.

The blackbird stood on the side of the road about six feet in front of her. It stared at her with unblinking dark eyes.

"Shoo!" Christine said, waving her hands toward the bird.

It didn't fly away or even hop around. It might as well have been a statue.

She thought of swinging her book bag at the bird, but she didn't want to anger it so that it would fly at her.

Christine walked around the blackbird giving it a wide berth. It turned to watch her as she passed.

She traveled the quarter mile between her home on Graceham Road and the bus stop twice a day during the school year. She'd seen plenty of birds during that time; crows, robins, cardinals–once even a hummingbird had zipped by her–but she had never seen a bird act as odd as this one. Occasionally, a bird would fly near her and even land on the street, but it always flew off if she got too close. She didn't intimidate this blackbird at all.

She kept walking down the road. She couldn't let a stupid bird delay her.

Christine thought about the homework she had to do tonight. Her teachers at Thurmont Middle School had no shortage of papers and projects to assign her, but she was an eighth grader. Next year in the fall of 1974, she'd be a freshman in Catoctin High School, and she had to be ready. Tonight's assignments would take at least an hour to do, and her mother would set her down at the kitchen table with a glass of Kool-Aid and expect her to get to work when she got home. She hoped she could finish quickly enough to have time to go over to Marci Robertson's house and listen to the new Kool and the Gang, Bachman Turner Overdrive, and the Jackson Five albums Marci had gotten for her birthday. Christine especially enjoyed grooving to "Dancing Machine" by the Jackson Five.

She paused when she saw the pair of blackbirds standing on the side of the road staring at her. They stood in the grass not moving. Christine stopped and turned around. The bird that had dive bombed her still stood on the edge of the road not doing anything but staring at her.

Odd.

When she turned back to start walking, a cowbird stood in front of her so close she could have easily kicked it. She was tempted to do so, but it didn't seem right. Like the other birds, this one didn't hop around or peck at the ground. It just watched her. It wasn't doing her any harm or even annoying her. It was just …weird.

She stepped around the bird and kept walking, although now she walked faster than she had been. She wanted to be inside her house. She wouldn't have to see these odd birds there or feel their eyes upon her.

A half a dozen starlings landed on a power line that ran above the road. That was nothing unusual except they also stared at her.

Christine shook her head. She had to be imagining this. One bird might stare at her but not every bird she saw.

She hurried down the road until she saw the flock of blackbirds, grackles, cowbirds, and starlings sitting on the road. There must have been hundreds of them. They formed a thick line not only blocking the road but stretching a yard of more to either side of the road.

Christine stopped. She couldn't walk through the birds, although she might kick her way through them. She was beginning to doubt that though, as all these birds stood unmoving and staring at her. She wished for a car to drive up so she could hitch a ride. At this point, she didn't even care who was driving. Let the car drive right through this line of birds. They would either fly away or be flattened.

She hurried into the field next to the road, planning to go around the line of birds, but they all turned in unison and hopped to stay in front of her. Christine ran in the other direction, thinking she could move faster than the birds and get around them. They took flight to move quickly to block her path.

Christine couldn't be sure, but it seemed there were more birds now than before their short flight.

Then even as she watched, a flock of birds flew in from the direction of Thurmont. They swirled around overhead and landed around the young girl. Thousands of birds formed a solid circle around her that was six feet wide.

Christine turned, looking for a way through the line. It was too broad for her to jump over. She swung her book bag at the birds. They didn't move, and she knocked them over like bowling pins. The fallen birds flapped their wings until they could get their feet under them again.

Christine suddenly realized what made her so uneasy about the birds in addition to their staring. The birds that had fallen over hadn't made a sound, not when the book bag had toppled them and not when they had struggled to stand up. If Christine had been hit with a book bag, she would have yelled, and she was a lot bigger than a bird.

"Help!" she shouted, hoping someone in a nearby house would come out to help her.

Someone had to be nearby. She wasn't so sure what anyone could do to help her. If the birds wouldn't move for her, they wouldn't move for anyone else. Christine would feel easier, though, if she wasn't so out badly outnumbered. Not that 5,000 birds to two people was much better than 5,000 birds against just her.

"Help! Somebody help me!"

No one came, and no one was in sight. She was on her own.

Christine suddenly yelled and ran toward the outside of the line. She kicked at the birds and judging by the crunch she heard, she stepped on at least one of them. And still none of them made a sound.

She had only taken a few steps into the birds when they took flight and circled around her. Christine stood in the center of it all afraid to try and push through the swirling wall of birds.

"Help!"

She doubted anyone could hear her. She could barely hear herself among the beating of wings. Christine looked up at the sky in time to see the flying birds close the gap of sunlight.

Sarah Adelsberger stepped out from behind the blue spruce tree so she could see things better. The swirling flock of birds numbered at least 10,000, probably more. They spun in a tight circle as large as a house.

Even as she watched, the circle tightened and grew denser so that no flashes of daylight could be seen through the column. Then the birds shot off in all directions in a wild flurry.

Sarah walked across the field and crossed the street. She came to a stop where the column of birds had been. She saw a few spots of blood on the grass and a quarter-size piece of canvas from Christine's book bag, but that was all.

Sarah picked up the piece of canvas and put it in her pocket. Then she looked into the sky at the birds, most of which were specks against the sky as they flew off.

Somehow she knew they wouldn't go too far. They had come for a purpose.

CHAPTER 2: THE POWER

Sarah Adelsberger's hand trembled as the thirteen-year-old reached for the bottle of Coca-Cola on her aunt's kitchen table. She grasped the glass bottle with both hands and gulped down most of the soda until she thought a giant belch would explode from her throat.

Had she really seen thousands of birds attack another student from Thurmont Middle School? If not, then what had happened to Christine Weber? The birds had surrounded and covered her, and when they had left, Christine had vanished.

Sarah shivered and then smiled. It might be a terrifying image to recall, but Christine, her school tormentor, was gone.

A macaw landed on the table in front of Sarah. She jumped. It was just Francis, her Aunt Anna's pet bird. Unlike any pet bird Sarah had ever seen, Francis wasn't kept in a cage. He was allowed to fly around the house wherever he wanted. Amazingly, he always seemed to do his business in a sink or toilet. Aunt Anna insisted the bird wasn't trained, but birds didn't do that on their own, did they?

"Sarah, what's wrong?"

Her aunt had stood up from the table to get herself a piece of apple pie. Now she stared at Sarah from the counter.

"I saw something today. I think it was horrible, but I'm not sure if it really happened," Sarah said.

"Tell me."

So Sarah explained how she had followed Christine home after school to confront her and end Christine's bullying. Sarah had been standing behind a tree working up her courage to confront Christine when the birds had attacked, and Christine had vanished.

"Marvelous," Anna said when Sarah finished.

"Marvelous? Didn't you listen? Christine vanished!"

Anna nodded. "I heard you. It was your power protecting you."

Sarah shook her head. "My power? What power? What are you talking about?"

Anna pulled a chair nearer Sarah. She sat down across from her niece and held her hands. Anna Whitcomb was only 10 years older than Sarah, so they were more like friends than aunt and niece.

"I've been telling you that you have power. It runs in our family. If you have it, it makes itself known during puberty," Anna said.

Sarah's brow furrowed. This is what her aunt had been talking to her about since the school year had started? Sarah had just thought her aunt was a women's libber talking about the power of women in the 1970s.

But this… this was unreal. Yet, Sarah had seen it happen.

"Christine was a bully," her aunt said. "You told me so yourself."

Sarah nodded slowly. "Christine was picking on me again in school today, calling me a cow." Sarah was pudgy while Christine had hit puberty early and wore make-up so she looked like a high school prom queen. People said Sarah, her aunt, and Sarah's mother all looked like sisters. Sarah only hoped that in 10 years she would look like her aunt with her shapely figure.

"Your power acted to protect you from Christine," Anna said.

"But what about Christine?" Sarah asked. "All I found was a little bit of blood and a piece of her book bag."

Sarah pulled the piece of blue canvas of her pocket. She held it up for her aunt to see.

Anna smiled and nodded. "In that moment, you must have hated Christine for what she did to you, and your power worked through the familiars to take care of it for you."

"Familiars?"

"Your spirit animal. Familiars can use our power to aid us when we need it. In our family, birds are often our familiars."

Sarah glanced at Francis who was still sitting on the table seemingly following the conversation. He even nodded when Sarah looked at him.

"But how?" Sarah asked.

Anna stroked Sarah's hair. Their hair was the same color, but Sarah thought hers was stringy compared to her aunt's lustrous, raven-black hair. "That doesn't matter. All you need to know is that judging by the number of birds that responded to your need, you are very powerful, and that power will take care of any problems that threaten you."

Sarah knew her aunt meant to comfort her, but the comment scared her.

When Sarah's mother picked her up after she finished work, Sarah said nothing about what had happened to Christine. Aunt Anna had warned her that people who didn't understand the power would not believe her or even fear her.

At the dinner table with her parents, Sarah stared out the window at the birds eating from one of the feeders that her mom maintained in the backyard.

"It's late in the season for so many birds to be around," her mother said when she noticed Sarah staring out the window.

"Is it?" Sarah said, barely paying attention to what her mother was saying.

"It's November," her mother said. "Most of them should have flown south to warmer places."

"Why not all of them?"

"I guess they have a reason to stay. They're lovely, aren't they? I love to watch them fly. They are so free when they are in the air gliding along on nothing but an air current." Her mother sighed as she turned to watch three starlings hopping around on a bird feeder.

Later, after Sarah finished washing the dinner dishes, she put on a jacket and walked into the backyard to get closer to the birds.

She comes.

Sarah looked around but saw no one. "Who's there?"

Will you make us act?

She realized the voice was in her head, but it wasn't her voice. Then she saw a cowbird sitting at her feet. She held out her hand to the bird, and it flew up and landed on her palm. Sarah leaned closer and stared at the bird.

What would you force us to do this time?

"Is that your voice I'm hearing?"

Let us leave.

"Us? What? The birds?"

You are bad.

Sarah frowned. "What are you talking about?"

You force us.

"I don't force you to do anything."

You made us take the other one.

The other one must have meant Christine. She was the only one the birds had taken.

"I didn't make you take her. The power did." Sarah realized that she was arguing with a bird, but she couldn't help it. She felt a surge of anger come from nowhere.

You are bad.

"Then go!" Sarah yelled. "If you want to leave so much. Go!"

The cowbird flew off of her hand, its wings flapping furiously. Sarah thought it would fly away, but it flew full force into the side of the house. She heard a sickening thud, and then the bird fell to the ground.

The anger vanished.

Sarah ran over and scooped up the bird in her hands. It didn't move. She stroked its head gently.

"Don't be dead. Don't be dead," she said almost like a

chant.

The bird's head turned at an awkward angle. Its wings flapped, and suddenly it was standing in her hand.

"Are you all right?" she asked.

The bird stared at her, and Sarah realized that instead of black, the bird's eyes were a smoky white.

Fly now.

Sarah heard the voice, but it wasn't the same as the voice she had heard earlier. This one was deeper and sounded scratchy.

"It that you?" she asked.

Yes.

The bird flew off.

Had she brought the bird back to life? What was happening to her?

CHAPTER 3: UNFAIR EDUCATION

Sarah Adelsberger woke in the morning feeling tired rather than refreshed. She hadn't dreamed about the birds covering Christine Weber and the teenager not being there when the birds flew off. She hadn't even dreamed about bringing the bird with the broken neck back to life. She would have expected to have nightmares about those things because they had happened, but she had dreamed about something that hadn't even happened.

In her nightmare, she had argued with Mrs. Zentz, her science teacher at Thurmont Middle School. Sarah couldn't remember what they argued about, only that they had been shouting back and forth. While Sarah believed Mrs. Zentz didn't like her, the teacher had never treated Sarah as poorly as she had in the dream. The teacher made fun of Sarah's questions and laughed at her answers. She called Sarah a "stupid, fat girl." Sarah had also felt a lot angrier toward the teacher than she had ever felt in real life. Maybe it was because of the way the dream teacher acted, Sarah still seethed with anger.

She got herself ready in a fog. She dreaded going to school because she knew Christine wouldn't be there. Christine was a popular student, and people would wonder where she was. No one except Sarah's family would have cared if Sarah had gone missing.

At Thurmont Middle School, Sarah heard Marci Robertson say Christine was supposed to come over to her house after school, but Christine had never showed up. John Poole mentioned that Christine hadn't seemed sick yesterday, and she was probably playing hooky.

Most kids wanted to talk about all the birds. Thousands of blackbirds, grackles, cowbirds, and starlings had started arriving in the area yesterday, and only Sarah knew that she was the reason they had come. She didn't know how she had called them or how to make them go away, but her aunt had explained to Sarah that she had power.

Sarah walked into her science class and felt angry at the sight of her teacher, not for anything Mrs. Zentz had done, but because of how Mrs. Zentz's dream self had acted. Mrs. Zentz was a few years older than Sarah's mother, but not as old as Mrs. Smith, Sarah's English teacher who looked like a dried apple. Mrs. Zentz's straight, red hair had to be dyed as bright as it was, and her dark-brown eyes felt like daggers when they narrowed in on you. When Mrs. Zentz smiled at Sarah, all Sarah could do was frown.

During the lesson, Sarah heard some other students murmuring. She turned around in her chair to ask what was happening, and she saw a line of blackbirds and starlings perched on the windowsill. They all faced into the classroom, and they were all staring at Mrs. Zentz.

The teacher tried to ignore them, but she kept casting nervous glances over her shoulder toward the windows. Then she would stare at Sarah.

Sarah's bad dreams continued, and they wore the young girl down. As the weeks progressed, she became sullen and depressed. She lost her appetite and started losing weight. Ordinarily, the idea of losing weight would have delighted her, but she was feeling anything but happiness. Even the Christmas break didn't improve her mood. She still dreamed of Mrs. Zentz, but now, they physically fought each other in Sarah's dreams, punching, kicking, and pulling hair.

Sarah's father wrote off her attitude as one of the unpleasant symptoms of puberty. Her mother didn't seem as certain. She kept asking Sarah what was bothering her, but Sarah knew her mother wouldn't understand. Only Aunt Anna knew what Sarah was going through. She gave Sarah exercises to do to control her power. Sarah did them and felt she was making progress. Then she would try to make the birds leave, but instead, more flew into Graceham.

The longer the birds stayed, the more problems they caused. Dead birds abounded. People hit them with their cars. Other birds starved because there wasn't enough food for what was now estimated up to ten million birds. Chirping and shrieking kept residents awake at night. The birds coated the ground with their droppings.

When Christine never returned to school, the "playing hooky" story changed to her running away from home. This only seemed to make her even more popular because students thought she ran away to chase her dream to be a singer in New York City.

When spring arrived, Sarah's father often talked about the Frederick County Government's efforts to drive the birds off. County employees tried loud noises and explosions to scare the birds away, but it didn't work. Next, they tried thinning out the pine grove where many of the birds liked to perch, but that didn't work either.

Sarah had come to accept the birds and didn't mind them. If her aunt was right, they were here to help her. That brought her a small measure of peace of mind before her nightmares drove it away each night.

Sarah watched the birds sitting on the windowsill outside of her science class every day. The number of birds had increased so that they were jammed wing to wing on the sill. They all still looked into the classroom, and they all still stared at Mrs. Zentz.

"The birds must want to know more about science," Mrs. Zentz sometimes joked.

No one mentioned that hers was the only classroom where the birds gathered and that they were only there during Sarah's science class. Odd questions without answers no one wanted to ask.

Sarah still had no idea how to control the birds, which she

didn't mind so much now seeing how she had forced the cowbird to break its neck against a wall in November.

"Sarah?"

Sarah's head jerked around to face front. Mrs. Zentz had asked her a question.

"Pay attention," the teacher said. "I'm sure you've seen plenty of birds these past few months."

Although Mrs. Zentz still smiled, Sarah could tell having the birds only on her windowsill at the school concerned her. They didn't even land on the windowsills of the classrooms to either side of Mrs. Zentz's room. It worried her. Mrs. Zentz had become short-tempered since last fall, although she still wasn't as mean as dream Mrs. Zentz.

"I like watching the birds," Sarah said.

"Well, you can watch them when you're not in class. It's not like they're hard to find. Now please explain the process of photosynthesis to the class."

Sarah's anger surged. She wanted to scream and yell at the teacher. Instead, she controlled herself and said, "No." The other students whispered, "Oooooo!"

Mrs. Zentz put her hands on her hips. "No?"

"That's right."

"And do you have a reason for that?"

"I don't want to. I want to watch the birds."

"Then perhaps you'd like to watch them while you're in detention."

Sarah shook her head and turned away from her teacher. "No, I'll watch them now."

The teacher walked over next to Sarah's desk. "What has gotten into you, Sarah? You are being insubordinate."

"And you're being nasty and mean," Sarah said without turning back.

Mrs. Zentz slapped her desk. "Enough! Take your books and go to the office. I will call down and tell them to expect you."

Sarah stood up quickly, knocking over her desk chair. Mrs. Zentz jumped back, and Sarah smiled. She pulled her books out of her desk and stomped to the door to the class. She didn't even bother to pick up her overturned chair.

As she left, the birds pecked hard at the windows. When one of the panes cracked, some students yelled in surprise. It lasted only a few seconds until Sarah was out of the door and walking down the hall.

CHAPTER 4: VENGEANCE

Thirteen-year-old Sarah Adelsberger sat in silence beside her Anna Eichholtz as her aunt drove her new corvette along Main Street in Thurmont. Sarah had always enjoyed driving in her aunt's flashy cars, but not this morning.

The principal at Thurmont Middle School had suspended Sarah for three days for back talking and being insubordinate to Mrs. Zentz, her science teacher. The principal told Sarah she needed to calm down and get her priorities straight. She also had to apologize to Mrs. Zentz when Sarah returned to school.

That would not happen no matter how long they kept her out of school.

Aunt Anna had picked Sarah up from school because Sarah's mother worked in Frederick and couldn't leave early.

Her parents would have plenty of time to yell at her this evening, and Sarah had no doubt she would be grounded, too.

"Do you want to talk about it?" Aunt Anna asked.

"So, if I've got this great power, why didn't it protect me from getting suspended?" Sarah asked.

Her aunt had told her weeks ago that Sarah had some sort of power like a witch, but not a witch. Sarah wouldn't have believed her except for the birds she had apparently summoned to attack Christine Weber. The birds had kept coming to Graceham even after the attack and now the tiny town had millions of birds living in it.

"Maybe it will protect you," Aunt Anna said.

Sarah stared out the side window at the houses whizzing by. "How? I've been suspended already."

"But you aren't in danger from it… at least not yet."

Sarah turned to face her aunt. "So the power only protects me when I'm in danger?"

"Yes."

"Who decides when I'm in danger? The power?"

"You do."

"If I decided, then I wouldn't have been suspended. Mrs. Zentz would be…"

"Would be what?"

Sarah shrugged. "Nothing." *Dead*. She had been about to say, "Mrs. Zentz would be dead." Sarah didn't really feel that way, did she? She didn't like Mrs. Zentz, but the teacher had done nothing so bad Sarah should want her dead. What was wrong with her to think that?

"The power is strong in our family," Anna said. "Not everyone has it, but all those who have it are women."

Sarah frowned. "Am I a witch?"

"Yes, I guess you could call us that, but we're not quite witches in the way most women who practice witchcraft nowadays are."

"Why?"

"So many of them don't have the power. They are seeking it, but if they don't have it, they won't gain it. Our numbers have been growing because of the women's liberation movement, but most of those women becoming witches are angry feminists rather than true witches."

Sarah cocked her head to the side. "And we're real witches." It was a statement rather than a question.

"Yes, and if you choose, you can use your power to do good and protect yourself from those who have wronged you. Who has wronged you, Sarah? Who can you use your power against?" Anna asked.

"Does it always have to be against someone?"

Anna smiled. "Oh, yes, the only way to grow your power is to use it to dominate others."

Sarah's brow furrowed. That didn't sound right.

"I've been dreaming about Mrs. Zentz since Christine disappeared," Sarah said. "At first, we just argued. Now we fight in the dreams. I think she wants to kill me."

"She's your science teacher, isn't she?"

Sarah nodded.

"And she's the reason you're suspended?"

Sarah nodded again.

"Then I think your dreams are showing you how your power can help."

Sarah's brow furrowed. "By getting in a fight with her?"

"Not literally showing you, but it's showing you your power can help you like it did with Christine."

Her aunt made the S turn near the Moravian Church, which pushed Sarah against the door so that she was staring at the old church. She felt a wave of guilt.

"I don't know how I did that," Sarah said. "It scared me."

"You thought about her. You focused on her so your power could focus on her. Then you got rid of the problem."

Sarah's parents grounded her for a week and gave her extra chores as punishment. They also agreed with the principal. Sarah had to apologize to Mrs. Zentz.

On the last night of her suspension, Sarah dreamed of Mrs. Zentz again. They fought, but this time, Sarah killed her. As Sarah choked Mrs. Zentz to death, Sarah felt happy, euphoric even. When she woke up, she still felt ecstatic. The feeling disappeared when her mother drove her to school, and Sarah had to apologize to Mrs. Zentz. Rather than shake the teacher's hand, Sarah wanted to lunge at her and choke her. The feeling frightened her.

Sarah seethed throughout the day. It wasn't right that she should have to apologize. She had already been punished.

When the school day ended, Sarah rode the school bus home. However, she didn't get off at her stop. She continued on to Rocky Ridge, which is where Mrs. Zentz lived. Sarah had found her teacher's address in the telephone book. Sarah walked to the side of the small ranch-style home so that she couldn't be seen from the driveway.

Think about her. Focus on her, Aunt Anna had said.

Mrs. Zentz got home around 4:15 p.m. Sarah watched her car turn onto the driveway. She tried to stare at Mrs. Zentz through the front window of her Volkswagen Beetle, but the sun reflected off of it.

Think. Watch. Focus.

Sarah watched the birds flying towards her from all directions – crows, blackbirds, cowbirds, starlings, grackles. They landed and moved in close together to form a wide band of feathers around Mrs. Zentz and her car.

The car door opened and Mrs. Zentz stepped out. She looked at the staring birds and then glanced around. Was she looking for more birds or someone to help her?

Unconcerned, Mrs. Zentz started to walk toward her front door. The birds parted before her, but they weren't hopping away. They toppled over and slid out of the way without Mrs. Zentz even touching them.

More birds arrived and flew at the teacher, but they seemed to bounce off an unseen wall and fall to the ground. Another flock flew in and was rebuffed, but Sarah could see Mrs. Zentz was sweating. Whatever she was doing to keep the birds away was wearing her down.

Think. Watch. Focus.

More birds arrived and swirled around Mrs. Zentz. Then the birds flew up and joined the melee. Sarah couldn't see the teacher any longer. Too many birds were moving too fast.

Then the birds scattered, and like Christine, Mrs. Zentz was nowhere to be seen.

Sarah came out from her hiding place and walked over to where Mrs. Zentz had been standing. She saw no blood or scraps of material, but she also saw no sign of Mrs. Zentz.

What she did see was a patch of dirt. The grass had been pulled up to expose the dirt. A set of seven symbols had been drawn in the dirt in a circle. Nothing like that had happened when the birds attacked Christine.

What did the symbols mean? They weren't letters. Sarah had never seen anything like them.

Something told her they were wrong. They shouldn't be here. They hadn't been here before Mrs. Zentz came home. Now that they were, all Sarah knew was that they shouldn't be.

CHAPTER 5: TAKING POWER

The 12 women stood in the wooded clearing between Graceham and Thurmont. They all wore white cloaks with hoods that covered their heads. They talked quietly in small groups, paced, and looked at their wristwatches.

Finally, Anna Eichholtz stepped up to the small campfire burning in the center of the clearing. She slid the hood off her head.

"As I told you, Barbara isn't coming, I will lead the coven tonight," Anna said.

The other women stopped what they were doing and moved to stand in a circle around the fire.

"What gives you the right to lead?" Kate Montgomery asked.

Anna lifted her chin and stared at each of the other witches over the fire. "I removed Barbara, and she will not return. Now, as the most powerful among you, I claim the right to lead."

The other women murmured. Some of them turned to walk away.

"How did you do it?" Kate asked. "You weren't more powerful than Barbara. That is why she led this coven."

Anna raised her hand. A small starling flew from the trees and landed in the middle of the fire. The flames ignited the bird's feathers. It didn't move or screech in pain. The witches gasped. The bird toppled over. It was a blackened husk.

"I brought the birds to Graceham, and they killed Barbara," Anna said. "They will remain here to take care of anyone else who opposes me."

The birds. Anna didn't need to say more. Everyone knew of the millions of crackles, crows, starlings, and cowbirds that had been living in Graceham for months. They were a nuisance that no one – not even this coven – had been able to drive away. Now Anna had proclaimed that she controlled them, and she did, although it wasn't her alone.

Her niece, Sarah, might have the power, but Anna knew how to control that power and use it.

Sarah Adelsberger answered the knock at her front door. She opened it, and saw Mrs. Zentz standing there. Sarah stifled a scream. Her science teacher gave her a half grin.

"Well, that answers the question I had about whether you were involved in what happened to me," Barbara Zentz said.

Sarah stepped back and hung her head. She expected to feel angry like she had when she had seen Mrs. Zentz for the past few months. Instead, she felt ashamed like she had after she had killed Christine Weber.

But Mrs. Zentz was alive. How could that be? Sarah had seen her disappear beneath thousands of birds Sarah sent to attack her science teacher.

"How?" Sarah asked.

"There's so much you don't know, Sarah, and you need to know it," Barbara Zentz said.

"I know everything I need to know! You want to kill me!" Sarah tried to stir up her old anger, but it just wasn't there.

Sarah closed her eyes and tried to focus on needing protection. She called to the birds. They would come to protect her. They always came to her aid.

When she opened her eyes, Sarah saw only three birds had come, and they weren't attacking Mrs. Zentz. They sat on the ground staring at Sarah. Where were the rest? Millions of birds were all over Graceham right now. You could hardly take a step without stirring up a flock and only three had answered Sarah's call?

Sarah shook her head and said, "How did you stop them? How are you still alive? What are you?"

"May I come in? We need to talk."

Sarah looked around for more birds. Seeing none, she stared at her teacher. Mrs. Zentz took her silence as assent and walked into the house.

"Are your parents home?" Mrs. Zentz asked.

"Not yet," Sarah managed to say.

Mrs. Zentz nodded. "Good. This should be a private conversation. Do they know about what you can do?"

"No."

Mrs. Zentz raised an eyebrow like she did in class when she suspected a student was lying to her. "Even your mother?"

"No. Only my aunt knows."

Barbara walked into the living room and sat down on an armchair. Sarah stared at her. It had been three days since she had sent the birds to attack Mrs. Zentz. Sarah thought the teacher was dead, but she looked fine. She wasn't even scratched, although thousands of birds had tried to claw and peck her to death.

"Are you a witch?" Sarah asked.

"Yes, as are you apparently."

"That's what my aunt told me."

"Your aunt? Anna Eichholtz? She told you you are witch?"

When Sarah nodded, Barbara closed her eyes and held a hand out, palm up, toward Sarah.

"What are you doing?" Sarah asked.

Mrs. Zentz said nothing. Then she took a deep breath and opened her eyes.

"I can sense the power in you, but it's all raw power."

Raw power? Her aunt had never called it that. It didn't sound good.

"You have enough power to control the flock that that has been causing problems around here, but without the training, you couldn't keep them here for all this time. You don't have the focus to make the birds obey your will."

"My aunt trained me," Sarah blurted.

Mrs. Zentz pursed her lips. "Really? You tried to get the birds to attack me again at the front door, didn't you?"

"No!" Mrs. Zentz arched an eyebrow. "Well, I tried, but it didn't work," Sarah corrected herself.

Barbara nodded her head slowly. "You're being used by another person who has control, but not your power."

Sarah shook her head. "No, it can't be. Nobody else knows what I can do. No one was even there for what I did to you and Christine."

"Christine? Christine Weber?" Sarah nodded. "What happened to her?" Barbara asked.

"It was like what happened to you. The birds surrounded her and she disappeared. All that was left was some blood and a piece of her book bag."

Mrs. Zentz sighed. "Oh, Sarah, you're being used, and you don't even realize it. Your aunt is controlling your power. Your anger gave her a way in."

"No, my aunt has been trying to help me. I told you she's been training me."

"Sarah, you think you have control of your power, but you haven't shown the control needed to do what you think you have done. Your power is like the water in a fire hydrant and you're the hydrant. The water will pour out of you, but it takes control – the fire hose connected to the hydrant – to direct and use all of that water. Your aunt is the fire hose."

Sarah felt a knot in her stomach she didn't even realize was there uncurl itself. "Then I didn't kill Sarah?"

Barbara shook her head. "No more than the hydrant puts out the fire. Your aunt must have used an anger you felt toward Christine to find a way into your emotions and power. That gave her control over your power. Witches sometimes control another's power to help train them, but the trainee always knows what is happening so she feels how to control her power on her own."

"But she's my aunt."

Her aunt couldn't have used her. Aunt Anna was like her

older sister. She had watched Sarah every afternoon after school since Sarah was in Thurmont Elementary School. They were so close. Sarah told her aunt her secrets, her hopes, her worries. She had told her about Christine bullying her.

"She's also a witch with big ambitions but only moderate power," Barbara said.

"But she hasn't tried to control me. She has been helping me," Sarah insisted.

Mrs. Zentz reached out and patted her arm. "I'm sorry, Sarah. Calling the birds showed a great deal of control and experience, and you don't show that level of control. You called three birds to you, and they only sat at my feet."

Sarah stared at her in silence and then broke into tears. "Why! Why would she do this to me? I've had nightmares ever since Christine died."

Mrs. Zentz leaned over and hugged the young teen.

"It's your power. The young have great power, but I have never seen as much raw power as you have in you. Your aunt can use that power to control our coven, and with that, she could do just about whatever she might want around here. She has tried to take control before."

Sarah lifted her head. "What happened then?"

Barbara frowned. "Anna has only moderate power herself. I defeated her and took control of the coven when our last leader died."

"Are you going to fight her again? Are you going to kill her?" Sarah might not like what her aunt had done to her, but she didn't want her to die.

"I can't defeat her when she is using your power to sup-

31

plement her own. Even with the aid of the rest of the coven, I doubt it would be enough power. Even if I could, though, I wouldn't kill Anna. It's not my way, nor is the way of most witches. We practice a beneficial magic to heal and help others. I gain my power from the goodwill it creates. I work with nature. People want to see my spells succeed, which gives the spells more power than I have."

"That doesn't sound like the power my aunt talked about."

"It isn't. She fights against nature because she wants to control. If you swim with a river's current, you will swim faster because the current helps you. That is what I do. Your aunt swims against the current, working harder and believing she will make the current go in the direction she wants."

Sarah had tried swimming against the current on vacation at Ocean City. It could be hard work. She said as much to Mrs. Zentz.

The teacher nodded and stood up. "When you use the power the way your aunt does, you have control. You don't have to share with anyone. However, if you share your power, whomever has control has her power multiplied. By leading the coven, I have control of the power of all the witches in the coven. Your aunt will seek to control the coven because with their power and yours, she will be a match for any witch I know. She needs to be stopped."

CHAPTER 6: THE CHALLENGE

Thirteen-year-old Sarah Adelsberger said nothing when she arrived at her Aunt Anna's house in Graceham on the first warm day of 1973. She should have been happy or at least in a good mood with the 68-degree temperature and sunshine. She also knew she hadn't killed her teacher, and she wasn't responsible for her classmate Christine Weber's death either. It was a burden lifted from her conscience, but it had been replaced with another problem.

"What's wrong?" Aunt Anna asked as she mixed some herbs and spices to a stew cooking on the stove. She looked like a witch brewing a potion at that moment.

"Nothing," Sarah muttered.

"Sure seems like something's wrong. You're usually not so quiet. Are you having bad dreams again?"

The dreams of Mrs. Zentz, her science teacher at Thurmont Middle School, had seemed to real when she had them. Sarah knew now that they hadn't been her dreams at all, but projections meant to anger her.

"No, but…" Sarah looked her aunt in the eyes. "I suppose you already knew that!"

Anna Eichholtz stopped what she was doing and rinsed off her hands. "What are you talking about?" she asked as she dried her hands on a dish towel.

"I know about the dreams," Sarah said. "I know you used me."

Anna gave a light snort. "I don't know what you're talking about. I've never used you. I've tried to help you."

Sarah jumped up from her chair. "You tried to help you! You used me to get what you wanted."

She hadn't wanted to say anything to her aunt, but once she started everything started to spill out.

"What I wanted?" Her aunt smiled. It was a nasty smile Sarah had never seen on her aunt before. It scared her.

Her aunt said, "As I recall, you're the one who killed two people."

"No, I know that now! Stop lying!"

Sarah turned and sprinted from the house. She ran across a field to Hoovers Mill Road. Then she kept running until she reached her house.

Sarah's nightmares returned that night. Mrs. Zentz attacked Sarah and tried to kill her. It didn't anger Sarah now, though. Mrs. Zentz hadn't killed her when she had a reason to. She hadn't even been angry with Sarah for sending the birds to attack her, or rather, thinking she had sent the birds.

"I'm not afraid," Sarah told the dream Mrs. Zentz. "You're not real."

Mrs. Zentz opened her mouth and growled. Her teeth lengthened and sharpened. Her hair grew shaggy. Spikes poked out of her back, and her fingers lengthened into claws.

The sudden shift startled Sarah, but she quickly calmed down.

Then the dream monster attacked, and Sarah screamed.

Monica Adelsberger ran into her daughter's bedroom, still pulling her robe on. Sarah lay on her bed, thrashing and yelling in terror but still asleep.

Monica shook her daughter's shoulder. "Sarah, wake up. You're having a nightmare."

Sarah didn't wake, but she quieted down.

Monica patted Sarah's cheek. "Wake up, honey."

Sarah calmed somewhat at her touch. Then her eyes opened, and Monica saw her daughter's blue eyes had turned so pale that it didn't look like she had pupils.

Monica drew back sharply. She knew what this meant. She had seen it before. Something supernatural was in control of Sarah. It wasn't a demon or spirit, Monica had fought that type of possession before. It had to be another witch.

Sweat beaded on Sarah's brow, and her hands clenched into fists at her sides. Monica pulled sweat-dampened hair off her daughter's face.

"Don't be angry, sweetheart," she whispered into Sarah's ear. "Don't give into the anger. Release it. She can't control what isn't there."

Barbara Zentz startled the women of her coven when she walked into the clearing. Donna Eyler even screamed as if she was seeing a ghost.

Kate Montgomery looked from Barbara to Anna Eichholtz and back. "Anna told us you were dead," Kate said.

Barbara held her hands out to her side. "As you can see, I'm not. I've been… indisposed for a few days, but I'm back and ready to take my place among my sisters."

The women in the circle nodded, but Anna shook her head. "I lead the coven now."

"But you lied to us," Kate said. "You told us Barbara was dead."

"A slight miscalculation." Anna's light-blue eyes narrowed. "One that can be corrected."

"You aren't more powerful than me," Barbara said.

"I don't have to be. I have the coven's power."

Barbara had hoped Anna would give up her quest for power when she saw Barbara was alive. Unlike most witches who tried to work with nature rather than force it to their bidding, Anna would not give up her power now that she controlled the power of the witches in coven. The only way for Barbara to take back leadership of coven was for Anna to give up the power or for her to die.

"A coven is not for one person to control," Barbara said. "You lead a coven, otherwise, you are a thief not a witch."

Anna laughed. "You sound afraid, Barbara, because I've done what you are afraid to do."

"We won't let you control us!" Barbara shouted.

"I couldn't care less about you," Anna said.

She waved her hand, and Barbara grabbed at her throat. She dropped to her knees, trying to catch her breath.

"Do you understand now? Even if you had used your power against me, it is the power of one. I have the power of many."

Barbara knew what was coming and managed to throw up a shield, but when Anna's power hit, it still felt like being punched in the face. Barbara staggered back, but held onto the shield.

Anna struck again, and the shield broke with ease. Ease for Anna. It hurt Barbara so much she screamed.

Some of the other witches struck at Anna with different spells, but Anna's power included theirs. Her shields easily deflected the spells.

The fire in the center of the clearing flared, spitting out fireballs. The women ducked and rolled out of the way of the flames. Anna would have jumped out of the way, too, but her shields stopped the flames.

Then she saw Sarah shamble into the clearing.

Sarah was tired and her head ached, but she had pulled herself out of the nightmare with her mother's help. Now she had to stop her aunt.

"It's over, Aunt Anna," Sarah said. "Stop this before more people get hurt."

"Sarah, Sarah," Anna said in a soothing voice. "I am protecting you from people who would hurt you if they had the chance."

"I don't know these women. They aren't causing me pain." Sarah rubbed her temples. "You are."

"I can stop the pain."

Anna lifted her hand and threw Sarah backward. Monica ran out of the woods to help Sarah.

Anna laughed. "You shouldn't have come, Monica. This doesn't concern you. You walked away from this life."

"And you pulled my daughter into it!" Monica yelled.

Sarah threw her arm out, but nothing happened to Anna. Instead, a hard wind blew through the clearing nearly extinguishing the fire. Mrs. Zentz was right. Sarah had power, but she couldn't control it. She had never been trained.

Anna raised an arm in Sarah's direction. Sarah wanted to create a shield to block whatever her aunt would do, but she didn't know how. She felt her mother's hand on her back, and Sarah felt a shield form around the two of them. Although Sarah saw nothing, the shield felt oily for a few moments. Then the feeling vanished.

Anna's blue eyes widened. She frowned. "Poor, poor, Sarah. You must worry over whether the police will find out what you did to Christine. Did Sarah tell you she killed a girl,

Monica?"

Her mother didn't reply, or if she did, Sarah didn't hear it. She was caught up in a vision as if she was Christine Weber collapsing beneath the weight of thousands of birds. They clawed at her and pecked at her. Sarah screamed in pain, and a bird pecked at her tongue. She saw the birds. Many of them had their eyes closed as if they didn't want to see what they were doing. Amid the pain, she could feel a presence pressing on them from behind, forcing them to attack when they just wanted to fly away.

"No!" Sarah screamed, although she wasn't sure whether she said it or just yelled it in the vision.

She hurt all over. Her hair. Her toenails. How could Christine have endured all this?

"Stop, please stop," Sarah pleaded.

And the birds stopped. It was as if they were frozen in air. She wasn't free of them, but they had stopped the attack, which is what Sarah had asked.

Was she finally controlling the birds? Did she want to control them? Mrs. Zentz had said magic shared was more powerful than forced magic like her aunt held. The birds might not be witches, but they were influenced by magic.

"Can you help me?" she asked.

The answer came from far away not from the flock of birds surrounding her. *You can make us.*

"I don't want to do that. I want to stop the woman who is keeping you here."

Yes, we want to go, the voice said. Were the birds speaking to her as one?

"Then help me stop her."

We are afraid.

"I will give you the power to protect and control your-selves." Sarah thought she could do this. Her mother's touch had given her control without controlling her like Aunt Anna had.

"We would be free?"

"Yes, but first she must be stopped."

Sarah remembered her mother's whispered voice when she had been caught in the fevered nightmare Aunt Anna had created. *Release it. She can't control what isn't there.* Sarah had released the anger then and the nightmare faded. She tried the same thing now except with the power she felt with-in her.

She opened her eyes and dropped to her knees, suddenly weak. Anna still stood with her hand out to her sides. The other witches were on the ground. Sarah stood. She could feel her mother's hand on her back, soothing her and giving her control.

"You are strong, Sarah, but control is more important. Control allows you to take the power you want," Anna said.

"Not if I've already given it away," Sarah said.

The birds flew into the clearing. Anna shifted her stance, and Sarah could tell she had gone from attacking to strength-ening her shield expecting the birds' attack.

They didn't attack, though. They kept their distance fly-ing around Anna faster and faster. They started glowing red, but that shifted to orange, yellow, green, blue, and purple. Sarah wasn't sure she was actually seeing it until she heard her mother gasp.

"What's happening?" Sarah asked.

"I don't know," her mother said. "It's beautiful. They look magical."

As the colors shifted, the birds chirped and tweeted. It should have been a deafening chaos of noise, but the sounds blended so that Sarah could imagine it as a chant.

Inside the circle, Anna screamed, but the birds weren't close enough to harm her.

Are we free? the voice asked.

"I don't control you," Sarah said.

The birds flew off in all directions. Sarah was sure when she left the clearing most of the millions of birds that had been invading Graceham for the past few months would be gone.

Anna was gone, but the birds hadn't been close enough to attack. Yet, they had stopped her as Sarah had asked them to do.

She saw movement where her aunt had been. It was a crow left behind. Sarah walked over to the crow as it hopped around on the ground. Its wings didn't look injured, but it couldn't fly. Sarah was surprised only one bird had been injured in that swirling flock.

Sarah stopped near the crow, and it looked up at her with its blue eyes.

Sarah gasped and kneeled down closer to the crow. It didn't move away. It just stared at Sarah.

"Hello, Aunt Anna."

Who would have thought birds had a sense of justice?

CAST FROM THE GODS

CHAPTER 1: THE BOX

Nearly every morning in 1951, the sound of thunder – but no storm – woke anyone who tried to sleep late near Raven Rock Mountain. At first, the phenomena created curiosity until people realized that their newest neighbor – the federal government – was building under the mountain, something top secret.

No one was quite sure what it was, but the government

had taken over four properties in Adams County, Pennsylvania, along the Mason-Dixon Line that amounted to 280 acres including Raven Rock Mountain. Blasting into the mountain had started in January.

Occasionally, a few people gathered near the gate on Harbaugh Valley Road to watch the empty dump trucks enter the newly created hole in the side of the mountain and leave heaping with debris.

"I tell you, they're mining," Rob Fairbanks said as he watched a truck roll through the gate and onto the road.

"Mining what?" Don Parker asked. "There's no metals or minerals worth mining in there. Rock, yep, but they could get rock from a quarry. They're building something in there."

So the debate went with one side saying the government found something to mine, and the other side saying the government was building a secret installation. Occasionally, someone threw out an odd theory. The government was searching for something buried in the mountain. They were building a back way into Shangri-La, the president's hideaway a few miles away on Catoctin Mountain.

Whatever was happening, the trucks kept entering empty and leaving full.

A siren sounded, and a few minutes later, the debaters heard the thunder without rain. The mountain seemed to shake, but it could have just been the ground beneath their feet trembling. No tell-tale dust cloud rose into the air to tell you were there explosion occurred, and the mountain muffled much of the explosive sounds.

Bruce Nelson waited along with the rest of his work crew

outside of the entrance into the mountain. Powerful fans vented the cavern slowly forming beneath the mountain of dust-size debris.

He waited 10 minutes and walked into the cavern with his flashlight to check if the air was clear. It was hard enough keeping the area properly ventilated. He didn't need his men inhaling dirt floating in the air. He was the foreman on this project, so it was his call whether it was safe to re-enter the cavern.

No dirt and debris danced in the air reflecting his flash-light beam. He waved his crew in. Backhoes, bulldozers, and dump trucks disappeared into the ground. The backhoes were a new technology that certainly improved the speed of the job. The metal arms could reach into the debris and lift out large boulders that just a few years ago would have needed to be broken up.

What had been a solid mountain only a few months ago was slowly being hollowed out by the federal government. Each day the cavern grew larger as different work crews excavated toward the center of the mountain and hundreds of feet belowground.

Bruce wasn't entirely sure why he was being tasked to build this cavern, but the pay was good.

He watched a backhoe remove a ton of newly created debris and drop it into the back of a dump truck. When the truck was full, Bruce waved at the driver to head out and dump his load. He walked over to look at the pile of rock and dirt to see whether anything still needed to be broken down to smaller rocks. The next truck backed into the spot vacated by the first truck.

Kleig lights shone on the pile so that the backhoe operators could see what they were doing. The pile of rock was at least fifteen feet high inside a cavern that was forty feet tall and growing.

Bruce tread carefully. He didn't want to twist an ankle or start a rock slide. A boulder caught his attention and he knelt down beside it. It looked like the point of a three-sided pyramid. The edges were sharp and the sides smooth unlike any other piece of rock in this cavern.

He grabbed it in his gloved hand and tried to tug it loose. It didn't give. He brushed away some of the surrounding debris and saw that the sides continued to grow wider. The smoothness also continued. How could a rock shear so cleanly on three sides?

Bruce leaned closer to rock. Something about it was odd. He took his canteen from his belt and splashed some water on one side. The dust washed away, and the boulder gleamed. It was metal. Then it dawned on Bruce what he was seeing.

He stood up. "I need the rock breakers over here!" he called.

Half a dozen men walked over, carrying shovels and picks. Bruce pointed to the exposed metal.

"I need you to free this metal box," Bruce said.

"How did a metal box get in here?" Harv Worthington asked.

"What's in it?" Joe Jeffries added.

No one asked the question bothering Bruce. What sort of metal could withstand having all that debris fall on it and still appear smooth and unflawed? It had no pitting or scratches.

Bruce stepped back and let his crew get to work. It took them about an hour to uncover the box. Even free of debris covering it, the box was too heavy for 10 men to lift. It was roughly 12 feet long and four feet wide and two feet tall. The measurements were the only thing rough about it. It was smooth all over except for some odd characters on the side of the box.

He had men bring in buckets of water to rinse off the box. With the dirt gone, Bruce could see a thin seam that ran around all four sides a few inches from the top, although he couldn't see hinges or a lock.

Bruce pointed to the markings on the top. They were a series a straight lines, wavy lines, and dots. If not for the wavy lines, he would have thought it was Morse Code, which he had learned in the Army during the war.

"Anybody know what these are?" he asked.

"Hieroglyphics?" Joe suggested.

"They use pictures," Bruce said.

"They aren't letters," Patrick O'Hearn said.

"I know that."

Patrick shook his head. "No, I mean letters like the Chinese use."

Jack Standing Bear bent over and ran his fingers across the characters. His brow furrowed, and he jumped back.

"Recognize them?" Bruce asked.

The Cherokee shook his head. Then he turned and walked away.

Bruce didn't believe him, but he couldn't do anything about it. He turned back to the box. "It looks like it has a lid. Help me pry it off," he said to no one in particular.

He took a pick from Harv and used the blade as a lever. He tried to wedge it into the seam, but he couldn't get it to hold. After the third try, Bruce threw the pick down in frustration.

"What do you think's inside?" Harv asked.

"What else? Treasure," Peter Montgomery replied.

"We're not going to know until we get that lid off," Bruce told them.

He walked over to the backhoe operator, talked to him for a minute and walked back to the waiting crew.

"Step back," Bruce said. "I'm going to have the backhoe open it."

The backhoe arm first tried breaking through the top of the box, but nothing happened. The arm didn't even scratch the surface. Then it lifted the edge of the box and dropped it, hoping to jar the lid loose. Again, nothing happened. Finally, the backhoe turned the box on its side and hit the lid repeatedly.

The seam widened.

The backhoe tipped the box back. Then it scraped along the side of the box, trying to catch the seam. Bruce had his men wedge their picks and shovels into the seam trying to widen it.

With a whoosh, a hard wind blew out from the box, carrying with it a foul smell. The men staggered back under the force of the wind.

"What was that?" someone shouted.

Bruce approached the box slowly. The lid had come loose and lay slightly askew. He tried to push it aside, but it was too heavy.

"Help me with this," he called.

The crew of men grabbed the edges of the box and together they managed to open the box enough to they could see inside.

Bruce pulled a flashlight from his belt and turned it on, so that he could clearly see what was in the box.

He wished he hadn't.

CHAPTER 2: THE SKELETON

"An ill wind blows no good."

That old saying rang in Bruce Nelson's head when he and the men of his work crew opened the large metal box they had unearthed digging into Raven Rock Mountain on a government project. The wind that had burst outward when the seal on box lid broke had chilled him to his core.

Bruce hesitated to look inside the box. It suddenly seemed ominous, or at least worrisome to him. He wasn't sure he wanted to see what could generate such a wind.

Bruce switched on his flashlight and shone it inside the metal box. Bones gleamed under the light.

It was a skeleton. So the metal box was a coffin. That had been his first thought when he found it, but it hadn't been the right size for a coffin or made from the right material. For that matter, being located hundreds of feet underground wasn't the right place for a coffin.

Yet, he was staring at bones. At least he thought they were bones. As Bruce moved the flashlight beam up and down along the bones, he realized this was no typical skeleton.

"Is it a time capsule?" Harv Worthington asked from behind him.

"I hope it's a treasure," Joe Jeffries countered.

Without taking his eyes off the skeleton, Bruce said, "It's bones."

"Bones? No, that means we'll be delayed while the egg-heads come in here to study them," Harv said.

Bruce turned off the flashlight. "Help me pull the lid all the way off. There's something wrong with these bones."

The half dozen men on the crew struggled to lift the lid. It felt like it weighed more than lead. The effort left them all sweating and breathing hard.

"Careful," Bruce cautioned. "If we damage this, the high-er-ups will have our heads."

He thought it was more likely the lid would damage one of his work crew by smashing a finger or dropping on some-one's foot.

With the lid off, more light from the klieg lights could shine in the box. The skeleton was at least seven-feet tall. The arms were long, reaching down to the knees, which were reversed like many animals. The chest was broad, nearly as wide as the four-foot-wide coffin. The skull had a pro-nounced jaw filled with jagged teeth that seemed longer than they should be. It wasn't smooth along the top either. It had a series of small, horn-like growths all over the skull.

"What the hell is that?" Patrick O'Hearn said.

Bruce shook his head. "It's not human."

"You think?" Joe said. "Nothing human or animal has ever looked like that."

"Something did. There's its skeleton," Harv said stabbing his finger toward the skeleton.

Bruce rubbed his face. He would definitely have to call this in.

He kept trying to imagine what a creature with this skeleton would look like. He could almost understand why someone would want to bury it deep in the ground, even if he couldn't figure out how it was done.

"It has to be a fake like something for Halloween," Patrick said. "It doesn't even have skin."

Bruce stared at the skeleton again. Patrick was right. When Bruce was younger, he had worked at a cemetery helping dig the graves. One summer, the maintenance crew had needed to exhume a body for a police investigation. When the casket had been opened, teenage Bruce had seen the body. It had been dessicated with some spots where he could see bone, but there had been flesh and clothing. This skeleton had none of that. It was just bones that were clean and white as if they had never held flesh.

He shined the flashlight in the box. He saw nothing indicating anything but bones had ever been inside.

Fake or not this was above his pay grade.

Bruce told his men to take lunch, even though it was only 10 a.m. Then he went to the construction office at the entrance to the mountain to make a call.

The small caravan of cars arrived around noon. One held a general and colonel. His supervisor Paul McNeill was in the second car, and Dr. Howard Buchanan was in the third.

As the men climbed out of their cars, Paul hurried over to Bruce.

"Are you sure about this?" Paul asked.

Bruce nodded. "I wasn't the only one who saw the box or

the bones. Who would have buried something so deep?"

"I don't really care. My butt is not on the line over the who. We just need to make sure whatever you found is not damaged."

Bruce looked over at Dr. Buchanan. The man was middle aged with a receding hairline. He had the look of a former military man, and Bruce would have bet he was also a vet of the war. He was also the person in trouble over all this because he had verified the site as not being claimed as a religious site or graveyard by any Native American or pioneer group.

"I don't think what we found is something anyone can blame the doc for," Bruce said.

Paul rolled his eyes. "It's the government. They'll want to blame someone, especially if the news gets out we unearthed some Indian's great-great-great-grandpa."

"That's what I mean," Bruce said. "It's not Indian. I don't even think it's human."

The military men and Dr. Buchanan stopped talking and walked over to Bruce. He loaded them into a truck and drove to the rubble pile in the cavern. He walked them over to the box and shone his flashlight on the skeleton.

The colonel started laughing. When everyone looked at him, he said, "Well, it's obviously a hoax."

"I thought that at first, too," Bruce said. "But then I thought about the box. I'm not sure what that metal is, but it wasn't scratched even with tons of rubble falling on it. It's also so heavy it would have taken a heavy-duty truck to bring it here, and that would have been noticed."

Dr. Buchanan reached into the box and ran his hand

along a bone. "They feel real enough, although they look bleached rather than aged."

He walked around the box, stopping only when he saw the scratching on the box.

"Not that I know every language, but I don't recognize these characters, although my gut says it is a language of some sort."

"We had an Indian on our crew. When he saw those scratches, he just turned around and left," Bruce said.

Dr. Buchanan stood up. "I want to get some photos of those marks. Then I'll get the members of the language department at the university to look at them. Maybe one of them will recognize the symbols."

"What about the bones?" The general asked.

"Leave them alone for now until we know if a group will claim them. We have already disturbed them enough."

Bruce was happy enough to leave the bones alone for now, but he doubted any group would want to claim them.

Bruce drove onto the job site the next day, hoping that he could get back to the work. The best outcome would be that the higher-ups determined the skeleton was a fake. Then it could be thrown in the trash and work could resume.

He drove down the long tunnel and parked his truck. He made sure the windows were rolled up. This was to make sure no dust and dirt got inside the truck, although it always seemed to find a way in.

No one else was at the site yet. He walked over to the box, carrying his morning coffee in a Thermos. He took a swig of coffee to help clear his head, and he looked in the box.

He spit out his coffee and dropped the Thermos.

The skeleton was still in the box, but now it had flesh on it, at least on some of it.

"This is not good," Bruce muttered to himself. "This is not good."

Bruce grabbed his flashlight and shined the beam on the skeleton. The left foot now was covered across the top with gray fur. A red muscle now attached itself to the knee and upper right thigh. Leathery skin covered a hip and some new tissue beneath it. Black fur with white stripes covered part of the chest. More leathery skin covered the skull, which made the bone protuberances look even more like horns. A strip of scales ran along one arm.

Bruce started to turn away, but he stopped and stared at the new additions to the skeleton. He recognized the fur. It came from a gray squirrel, and the white-striped fur was skunk. The scales appeared to have come from a snake. He couldn't place the leathery skin, although it might have been from a bat. Where the skin and tissue touched, it seemed fused together.

Bruce took his pocketknife from his pocket and used it to move the skins. Not only were they connected to each other, they were connected to the skeleton.

He spun away and ran back to his truck.

CHAPTER 3: THE PIECES

Bruce Nelson was more than happy to allow the so-called experts to crowd around the odd metal box Bruce's work crew had unearthed hundreds of feet under Raven Rock

Mountain. The U.S. government had hired him to excavate a chamber under the mountain, not deal with metal boxes that couldn't be scratched and bones growing flesh.

Not just any flesh either. Patches of skin, fur, and organs from a variety of creatures covered the deformed skeleton he had found in the box. He didn't know how it had happened. He just wished he was constructing an office building in Baltimore and not some top secret chamber in what seemed to be a haunted mountain.

More than one egghead poking and prodding the skeleton proclaimed it a hoax, but none of them could explain how the bones came to be under the mountain or how the flesh had attached itself to the bones.

The eggheads increased the number of guards at the entrance tunnel and left, satisfied the foolishness would end. They thought locals had snuck into the tunnel and pulled a practical joke. Idiots! Whatever this box and skeleton might be, they weren't a hoax. Not that it mattered to him. He just wanted to get back to work.

The next morning Bruce drove a truck through the tunnel to inspect the work site before the day's work began. He didn't want to look in the metal box, but he knew he had to confirm the skeleton was undisturbed. If it was some sort of Indian burial, the government would be in enough trouble for opening the box. They wanted to leave the skeleton alone until they knew one way or another what was going on.

Bruce looked in the box and shook his head. Even more fur and flesh covered the skeleton, which now resembled a decaying corpse rather than a skeleton. The insides were filling out with a variety of organs. He leaned closer. The older flesh had changed. He remembered what it had looked like, but now it was gray and leathery and covered with short brown hair.

The site manager–a major from Fort Ritchie–threw a fit when he saw the skeleton. He chewed out the night guards, who swore no one had entered the chamber.

That evening, in addition to the guards at the entrance to the mountain tunnel, Private Jacob Parkinson drew guard duty for the metal box his fellow soldiers called "the coffin."

Jacob was stationed at Fort Ritchie on nearby South Mountain. He'd been working at Raven Rock since the excavation began. Like pretty much everyone else at Fort Ritchie, he had no idea what was going on under the mountain. The rumor mill said when the Russians detonated their own A-bomb a few years ago, it had spooked the top brass in the U.S. government. President Truman had ordered the construction of what would be a giant bomb shelter, but who was it for? It was out in the middle of nowhere.

In his five months on site, Jacob had never even been inside the mountain before tonight. He paced around the box. The first thing he had done after coming on duty was to look inside at the deformed skeleton covered with pieces of other animals. How could he resist?

Sergeant Collins had told him to watch over the skeleton and make sure nothing happened to it, as if grave robbers looked for graves hundreds of feet underground. And who would want a patchwork skeleton like he was looking at?

Jacob circled the perimeter at the edge of the light the

klieg lights cast. He picked up rocks and threw them at boulders protruding from the rubble pile. He sang to himself. This wasn't like walking along the fence line outside of the mountain. This cavern was too quiet, and there were no stars. Just light and darkness. Outside, he could listen to the night noises when he walked. He heard nothing in this space. Nothing lived here.

It was after his dinner break that Jacob started hearing noises. Maybe it was because he was feeling full after eating the roast beef sandwich and pretzels he had packed. He wasn't singing or throwing things. He was as quiet as the cavern, except the cavern wasn't quiet.

He could hear small rocks being dislodged and the scrape of claws along the rocks. He unslung his rifle from his back and let it hang loose in his hands. He kept his back to the coffin and tried to hear from where the sounds were coming. Easier said than done. Everything echoed in the cavern.

Jacob faced in the direction of the cavern opening, which was the most likely direction anything would approach from.

He waited.

A copperhead crawled across the cavern floor in his direction. Where had it come from? Copperheads needed warmth to control their body temperature. Why would a snake crawl half a mile underground? How long had it been crawling?

The snake moved his direction. Was it seeking the warmth of his body heat? Jacob stepped to the side, shouldered his rifle and drew his pistol. He didn't want to shoot the snake, but he also didn't want it crawling around where he might not see it before it bit him.

The snake didn't change direction. Instead, it continued in a straight line to the coffin and crawled inside.

Jacob moved up next to the box and shined his light inside. He couldn't see the snake. Where had it gone? Where could it have gone? Jacob hadn't seen it crawl out. He moved his flashlight to look around the outside of the coffin, but then he shifted his light back. Something was different. He stared at the skeleton and then realized what had changed. It now had a four-inch-wide strip of snake skin around its neck. What's more, that skin seemed to float in place as if resting on something Jacob couldn't see.

He unslung his rifle and pressed the end of the barrel into the space between the neck bone and the snake skin. The barrel passed through air.

As Jacob stepped back, a golden retriever jumped into the coffin. Jacob yelped and stumbled backward. He hadn't seen a dog in the tunnel. How had it gotten past the guards at the entrance?

"Get out of there, boy!" Jacob said, making a shooing motion with one hand.

The dog sat on the skeleton and whimpered. Then its skin slid off its body and onto the skeleton. The whimpers grew louder. The dog shimmered with a blue light.

Jacob felt his roast beef roiling in his stomach as he looked at the skinless dog. Then pieces of the dog's flesh slipped onto the skeleton. Before Jacob could retch, the dog disappeared.

Confusion replaced nausea. Where was the dog? What had happened to it? He shined his flashlight in the coffin, but he saw nothing of the dog except that its golden fur now covered the skeleton's right leg.

Jacob turned away. He grabbed for the walkie-talkie on his belt, but his hand froze before he could touch it. He turned toward the coffin and stepped into it.

No! He wanted to scream and thrash, but he couldn't. All he could do was whimper... like the dog.

No! No! No!

He looked down at the skeleton and saw it was glowing blue so brightly that Jacob couldn't see the bones beneath of the shape of the creature formed from the light.

His skin ripped and slipped from his body. He felt no pain. Jacob wasn't sure what surprised him more. That or seeing his skin spread across the skeleton.

He felt tugging on his thighs and chest and saw organs and muscle fall onto the skeleton.

Jacob wanted to scream, but all he could manage was a whimper.

And then he was gone.

CHAPTER 4: THE CAGE

The deformed skeleton was no longer a skeleton. As unusual as that was, it was only the second thing the soldiers noticed when they entered the excavated chamber under Raven Rock Mountain. The first thing they noticed was that Pvt. Jacob Parkinson, who had been stationed in the chamber to guard the skeleton, was missing. They called out his name and searched the around the piles of rock and dirt in case falling debris inside the chamber may have injured or even killed him.

The private was nowhere to be found.

"Do we have an AWOL soldier?" Maj. Henry Owens asked.

"I doubt it, sir," Sgt. Zachary Konrath said. He was Parkinson's squadron commander at nearby Fort Ritchie. "Private Parkinson seemed fine when he went on duty. He was a friendly soldier who was doing fine in the military. Even if he went AWOL, where did he go?"

Major Owens scowled as he looked around the dark chamber. "If I knew that, I wouldn't be standing here."

"No, sir, I mean, we had two men stationed on either side of the entrance to this chamber and other guards regularly patrolling the fence around this site. No one saw Parkinson last night."

"He must have snuck by you because he certainly isn't in here." The major waved his hands around to show he was talking about the cavern.

Konrath shook his head. "With all due respect, sir, I don't see how. Besides the guards, the entrance was well lit. My men would have seen someone leaving."

"It's happened before."

Sergeant Konrath stiffened. "Not with my men, sir."

Since construction of the underground complex had started, curious people had managed to get onto the property. A few made it as far as the entrance to the tunnel before they were caught. It wasn't as if those people had made it onto the property without being detected. They had been detected and caught before they breached the sensitive area. They had only gotten that far because the fencing had not been fully erected at the time.

This cavern was supposed to be an atom bomb shelter for

the government should the Soviets attack. It was nowhere near being complete yet, in part, because the chamber was being hollowed out of greenstone granite. Yet, a long time ago, a group of people using primitive tools apparently buried a mysterious coffin containing a deformed skeleton hundreds of feet below the ground. So far, no one could identify what sort of creature the skeleton had been when it was alive because it certainly wasn't human. They couldn't even identify the metal the coffin was made from, but strange things had been happening around it ever since the work crew had opened it.

"There's something else you need to see concerning the skeleton, sir," Sergeant Konrath said.

"I've seen the skins on the bones, sergeant," Major Owens told him.

Sergeant Konrath shook his head. "No, sir, this is something we discovered this morning when Private Parkinson's relief came in."

They walked over to the 12-foot-long and four-foot-wide and two-foot-tall coffin. Sergeant Konrath turned on his flashlight and shone the beam inside the coffin. The creature was nearly entirely covered with either fur, skin, or feathers of other creatures or the gray, leathery skin the other skins seemed to turn into. The face was gray with a wolf-like snout. However, instead of nostrils, the snout had a set of what appeared to gills running along its sides. The head resembled a sea urchin with spines growing from the top of it instead of hair.

Major Owens leaned over. "It looks different from yesterday. There's more flesh. It's barely even a skeleton now. I still couldn't tell you what it is, though."

"Sir, it's breathing."

59

"What!"

The major leaned over the coffin, staring at the creature's chest. As he watched, it slowly rose as the creature inhaled.

He straightened up. "Holy, Mother of God!"

"Is it alive, sir?" Konrath asked.

"How should I know? I don't even know what it is. How long has it been doing that?"

"At least since we got here at 0700."

Owens thought for a moment. "I've got to make some calls. I will send down four more men, fully armed. I want the men already here and the additional men guarding this... thing."

The major walked back to his Jeep. He drove out of the tunnel to the site office. He ordered the additional soldiers into the tunnel and then he placed a call to Dr. Howard Buchanan, the professor who had verified the site as not being claimed as a religious site or graveyard by any Native American or pioneer group. Howard arrived two hours later, and Major Owens drove him into the tunnel.

Dr. Buchanan looked at the creature in the box and said, "Amazing."

"Is that all you have to say?" Owens asked.

"What do you expect me to say? Somehow a skeleton is regrowing its lost organs and flesh. It's unheard of."

Owens sighed. He would have been a lot happier if Buchanan had been military. "I want to know: 1) What is it? 2) Is it alive? And 3) Is it dangerous? And not necessarily in that order."

Dr. Buchanan straightened up. "I'm afraid I can't answer any of those questions. However, one of my colleagues thought the characters etched on the coffin looked familiar. He is attempting to decipher them for me."

"Then I need to take some precautions." Owens looked around. "Sergeant Konrath, where are you?"

The sergeant hurried over. "Yes, sir."

"I want you and the other men here to put that lid back on the coffin. I will send a work team down here to erect a cage around it."

"Don't you think that's an overreaction?" Dr. Buchanan asked.

Owens poked the professor in the chest. "You just told me you can't tell me what this is or even if it's alive. Yet, I have a skeleton regrowing its body. So, no, I don't think I'm overreacting."

The 10 soldiers managed, with effort, to push the lid back into place. When it dropped into place on top of the coffin, the sound of metal on metal echoed back and forth in the chamber.

As the sound died off, another sound replaced it. It sounded like thunder or a deeply muffled growl.

CHAPTER 5: THE ESCAPE

Every soldier in the secret chamber beneath Raven Rock Mountain heard the roar from inside the metal coffin they had just sealed. It was a low, rumbling sound that rose to an anguished scream. Some soldiers covered their ears because, even deafened by the containment in the coffin, the roar was both loud and grating.

Almost unconsciously, they all stepped away from the coffin.

"What the hell was that?" Maj. Henry Owens asked to no one in particular.

Dr. Howard Buchanan shook his head. He was supposed to be the man who knew all the cultures of this region. He could speak at length about the settlers, Indians, and even proto-Indians who had lived in this area tens of thousands of years ago. He knew the flora and fauna. He had even studied the fossil evidence of the life that had once existed here.

"I don't know," the doctor said.

Something banged against the inside of the casket. A fist? A foot?

The truth was Howard had never heard of anything like this before. The men building this chamber had found the coffin three days ago. At that time, it had contained only a skeleton, which had been unusual enough seeing as how the coffin had been found hundreds of feet underground and the skeleton appeared deformed. Then the skeleton had start growing flesh and organs.

"I need to do research," Dr. Buchanan said.

"You researched this area before we started building," Major Owens said. "How much more can you find out? Don't you think the world would have heard about something like that?" He stabbed a finger in the direction of the coffin. "We need to know what we're dealing with now!"

"I can't tell you anything right now."

Another bang from inside the casket. Whatever it was, it didn't seem strong enough to lift the lid off. Not surprising, seeing as how it took nearly a dozen men to put it back on the coffin.

"Sergeant Konrath!" Owens called. The young sergeant

ran over and saluted. "I want additional security in case that… thing gets out."

Konrath looked at the casket. "All we have is fencing"

"Surround it with fencing and close off the top. Then surround that with razor wire. It probably won't stop it if that thing gets out, but it will at least give us time to shoot it to hell."

The sergeant sent three soldiers in the Jeep to the surface for supplies.

He returned and said, "My men will be back in a few minutes. Do you really think it will be needed, sir?"

As if to answer the question, the lid of the casket scraped a bit, and the soldiers brought their rifles to their shoulders.

The men returned with the chain-link fencing and razor wire. They set it up around the casket, bring the top ends together so that it resembled a see-through teepee when it was finished. They also hammered spikes into the ground to anchor the fencing. However, if the creature managed to lift the lid of the casket, the fencing wouldn't hold it for long.

Owens left to call his commander and update him on the situation. Dr. Buchanan left with him to return to Washington to try to figure out what they this creature was.

When Major Owens returned, he brought two more soldiers with Browning Automatic Rifles. The soldiers set up along one side of the casket and settled down to watch and wait.

The creature continued to growl and scream from time to time. Occasionally, it smashed at the sides, causing the soldiers to jump each time.

Additional men and equipment were placed at the entrance to the tunnel into the mountain. Major Owens wasn't sure what would happen, but he knew whatever was in that chamber had to be contained. He had ordered a steel cage to be brought in. He would feel a lot safer once that casket was behind bars.

Around quarter after seven, the creature screamed, and the lid rattled. The soldiers tensed. The lid slid to the side until it tipped over the edge.

"It's opened the casket!" Owens shouted.

The creature rose up from the casket. Owens knew at a glance that Dr. Buchanan wouldn't find anything about it because no creature like this could have existed on earth without someone writing about it. It looked more like one of the monsters from the movies than a living beast.

It was at least seven-feet tall with a gray skin with black spots at random locations. Its head would have been too large for its body if it had been a recognizable creature. Spiky growths covered its head. It looked like a puffer fish, except it had a long snout with gills along the sides. When it opened its mouth to roar, Owens thought the teeth resembled the flat, hooked appearance of shark's teeth.

The roar was deafening without the casket muffling the sound. It echoed off the walls of the chamber, making it sound as if the soldiers were facing an army of creatures, and one was more than enough.

It grabbed the fence with stubby fingers tipped with long claws. The fencing rattled and moved, but the stakes in the ground held... for the moment.

Owens backed away from the fencing.

"Shoot it!" Owens ordered.

Bullets ripped through the air, and the noise grew even worse, if that was possible. It was so loud that everything seemed to vibrate inside the chamber. The creature flinched as the bullets hit it, and pieces of its new flesh ripped away. But it remained standing and screaming.

Owens held up his hand, and the shooting stopped.

The creature grabbed the fence with its clawed hands. It didn't shake it, it stood staring at the soldiers. Then it closed its eyes, breathed in deeply and began glowing blue.

"What the…" Owens said.

He waved for the soldiers to step back. He had no idea what was happening, but he doubted he wanted to be close to it. All the soldiers moved back except for Private Bucknell, who stood staring at the creature. Then he took a step towards it.

"Private Bucknell, back away. Now!" Owens shouted.

The young man didn't. He took a step closer.

The creature opened its eyes and focused on Bucknell.

The soldier's back arched, and his head tilted back as if he was in pain. His body seemed to ripple beneath his uniform. Either that, or Bucknell was shaking in fear. He turned, and Owens gagged. The soldier's face was gone. All the skin on his face had vanished, and it was raw flesh staring at him, and then it all faded out of sight.

The creature inhaled deeply and Owens saw the pits and gaps of missing flesh fill in. The blue glow faded.

The creature growled. It grabbed the fence and pulled. A link snapped and then another.

"Fire!" Owens yelled.

The rifle fire opened up again. The creature flinched under the bullets, but it continued pulling at the fence. More links snapped.

If they could put enough lead into the creature, it would

have to stop again to rest and regenerate. Then what would happen? Would another soldier die? They had to get it to the point where it couldn't regenerate.

It had grown from a skeleton, though! How much more could they do to it?

"I want a slow retreat one at a time toward the entrance. We need to shore up the barricade."

One by one, the men stopped firing and ran toward the entrance to the tunnel, which was more than 100 yards away.

When all his men were gone, Owens took a hand grenade from his belt. He pulled the pin and let the handle fly. Then he lobbed it so it landed in front of the fence and creature, and he ran.

He counted as he ran and right before the explosion, he flattened himself on the ground to avoid any shrapnel.

He rolled over and looked back. He couldn't see anything through all the dust. However, he heard an angry growl and more metal snapping.

Owens pushed himself to his feet and ran for the entrance.

CHAPTER 6: THE ANGRY GOD

One by one, the soldiers stopped firing their rifles and ran toward the exit from excavated chamber beneath Raven Rock Mountain. It led to a half-mile-long tunnel that led to the surface.

When all his men were gone, Maj. Henry Owens took a hand grenade from his belt. He pulled the pin and let the handle fly. Then he lobbed it so it landed in front of the fence and creature, and he ran.

He counted as he ran and right before the explosion, he flattened himself on the ground to avoid any shrapnel. The explosion deafened him and he felt a pressure wave sweep over him.

He rolled over and looked back. He couldn't see anything through all of the dust. However, he heard an angry growl and more metal snapping.

Owens pushed himself to his feet and ran for the entrance. He could see his men parking trucks and Jeeps in front of the entrance to create a barrier. Machine guns were set up facing down the tunnel.

The men shouted and pointed. Owens glanced over his shoulder and saw a boulder flying out of the darkness.

He dove to the side as a rock the size of a foot locker hit the ground. It was heavy enough that Owens felt the ground tremble.

Owens made it to the parked vehicles as the creature appeared from the shadows. The soldiers firing at the creature. It stopped moving forward and roared. The bullets could stop its advance, but they weren't killing the thing.

As Owens made it to the other side of the barricade, a private ran up to him and saluted. "Sir, two men are at the main gate. They insist on speaking with you. One of them said he was a worker here. He says he has information about the box."

Anyone who knew the metal coffin was in the cavern must have been down there.

"I'll meet them. I want you to call up to Ritchie and get more ammunition sent down here. Also, have them send half a dozen men with grenade launchers," Owens told the private. Maybe the grenade launchers would be more effective at stopping whatever was trying to get out of the cavern.

The private saluted and ran off. Owens jogged down the road to the front gate where MPs kept all of the non-military people out. He saw two Indians standing with the MPs.

"Which one of you has information you think I need?" Owens asked.

The younger of the two men raised his hand. "I'm Jack Standing Bear. I was on the crew that unearthed the metal box. I recognized the inscription on the box and went to get this man. He is John Tamanend, an elder of the Susquehannock. They are the people who used to live in this area."

"If you saw the box, then you know it is not Indian."

Jack nodded. "The box is not, but the inscription was."

"What did it say? It was a warning saying the demon inside had been cast from the gods, and that the Old Ones, the people who lived in this land before the Susquehannock, managed to imprison it only at great cost. It should never be opened or the demon would be released."

Owens could see calling the creature a demon. It fit the bill.

"Well, it's too late for that."

The older man spoke and Jack translated. "He says there is a story told among his people of a god who fell to earth in a ball of fire. The god was angry and demanded the Old Ones worship him. Most did, but some did not want to worship an angry god. They didn't, and they vanished, but their numbers increased as more people resisted the angry god."

"How did they kill it?" Owens asked, looking over his shoulder back toward the entrance to the tunnel.

Jack translated and listened to the Tamanend's answer. "They didn't kill the god. You can't kill a god."

"Then how did they get it sealed in the box?"

"The warriors who fought the angry god tried many things. Arrows and spears could not kill him, no matter how many times they hit it. Many warriors attacked with knives only to vanish. In desperation, they ambushed the angry god, throwing oil on him and setting him on fire. This worked. Then the warriors took the bones and placed him in the metal box, which he fell from the sky in. We buried him as a god should be. He was placed in a deep chasm where he could rest peacefully and not be so angry."

Owens rubbed his chin. The firing started again. He knew it was only holding the creature at bay, but if the Old Ones could defeat it, so could the U.S. Army. He walked to the nearest soldier.

"Go to the camp. I need flamethrowers and cans of gasoline, as much as you can get a hold of quickly. Then get back here."

The soldier saluted and ran off. Owens turned to a corporal. "I need cans of gasoline and empty bottles. Meet me at the tunnel entrance."

Owens returned to the tunnel entrance as the firing slacked off. Then a boulder came flying out of the tunnel entrance. Then men scattered. The creature hid in the darkness and roared.

As the corporal and privates brought the cans of gasoline to Owens, he assessed his resources. He had 30 gallons of gasoline, a dozen empty pop bottles. The gasoline might be enough, but he needed more bottles. It would be at least an hour before he could expect the jeep back.

He had the bottles filled with gasoline. Men tore strips from their undershirts, soak them in gasoline, and stuff them mouths of the bottles. He had six soldiers take a pair of bottles and wait.

When the creature pressed again for the entrance, the soldiers lit their Molotov cocktails, ran forward and threw them at the creature. Half of the bottles missed. Of the six that did hit the creature, two hit too early. The creature knocked them away before they exploded. The four that hit the creature and exploded lit it on fire.

It roared in pain and thrashed around, rolling on the ground to put out the flames. It lay still. One of the soldiers slowly approached it.

"Get back here, private. We don't know if it's dead yet," Owens ordered.

The man didn't stop. Owens pointed to another private.

"Go bring him back."

The private ran out and started tugging on the other soldier's arm, but he wouldn't stop walking toward the creature. Then the creature glowed blue.

"Get away!" Owens yelled.

The second private started to turn back. He stopped as his skin split and vanished. Then both of the privates faded away.

On the ground the creature stirred.

And Owens was out of fire bombs.

The creature pushed itself to its hands and knees, lifted its head and roared. It looked barely affected by the fire. It hadn't been large enough, plus the two soldiers had aided its recovery.

He had to do something. It couldn't be allowed to escape the tunnel. No telling what damage it could do before they stopped it.

CHAPTER 7: THE BURIAL

Ancient Indians had killed the creature from the metal box once. The U.S. Army would have to do it this time. But the Indians hadn't killed it centuries ago. It had just been dormant. When the work crew digging under Raven Rock Mountain found the metal coffin two days ago, nothing but bones had been inside. Now, those bones formed a living monster that had killed four soldiers, and that number might rise exponentially.

Exploding Molotov cocktails had hurt it, but it had recovered from the fire. Now Maj. Henry Owens had no more bottles to use as bombs. Bullets slowed it down, but didn't stop it. If the creature reached the entrance to the tunnel and broke containment, there might be no stopping it.

The creature moved forward, swatting at the bullets as if they were annoying gnats. Owens could see the bullets tearing away bits of flesh, but most of the wounds glowed blue and healed themselves.

It would make it to the entrance.

He looked around, wondering if he could bring in more equipment to further block the entrance.

Owens saw the five-gallon cans of gasoline, but he had no bottles to fill with gasoline. He could use one as a bomb, but it would be too heavy to hurl accurately. The creature would have to come to the can. That wouldn't happen. It had no reason to, especially if it saw a burning fuse on the can.

Henry ripped off his shirt and pulled his undershirt off. He twisted the shirt into a thick cord and laid it on the ground. He grabbed one of the gas cans and doused the twisted shirt in gasoline.

Owens ran to the nearest Jeep. He unscrewed the gas cap and pushed the shirt into the Jeep's gas tank. Then he splashed the rest of the gas in the tank over the Jeep.

"Fall back!" he ordered his men.

The soldiers continued shooting as they moved backwards. Owens crouched behind the Jeep. Then he stood up, waving his arms over his head.

"Over here! Come here!" Owens called.

The creature roared and headed toward him. Owens wanted to run, but he held his ground and fired his pistol at the creature. When the clip ran out, he reached into his pocket and pulled out his lighter. He flicked the flame to life as the creature drew closer.

He leaned forward and lit his shirt on fire. It flared up and quickly disappeared into the gas tank.

Owens turned and ran. He heard the creature hit the side of the Jeep with a loud thump.

"Come on, come on," Owens muttered.

He looked over his shoulder. The creature reached down and lifted the side of the Jeep.

Then it exploded.

Owens threw himself face down on the ground. He felt the heat from the explosion. When it receded and he could hear again, he looked back. The burning creature thrashed around in pain, roaring loudly. It walked forward, but it did so slowly and without direction. It staggered and fell against a truck, catching the canvas covering the rear bed on fire. It roared once more and then fell to the ground.

Henry Owens stood up and stared at the bonfire of flesh and bones. It smelled like a giant barbeque. Then he remembered that some of the flesh burning was human, and his stomach turned.

He held his rifle at the ready, half expecting the creature to rise again.

The other soldiers moved closer. Some of them also had their rifles raised. Others just gazed at the burning creature, Owens thought they might under whatever trance the creature used to catch his prey, but they moved no closer to the fire.

He let the fire burn itself, which took a couple hours. He wanted to make sure as much of the creature burned as could. He wanted it to be only dust.

When all that remained was a smoking pile of debris, Owens walked around the pile. All the flesh had burned away as far as he could tell. He saw bones and metal from the Jeep. It surprised him to see all the bones intact. He would have thought the explosion would have shattered or at least broken some of them.

"This is not over yet."

Owens turned and saw Jack Standing Bear standing with the Susquehannock elder, John Tamanend.

"You mean it's not dead?" Owens asked.

"Perhaps dead as we know it, but can a god be killed?"

"It's just bones."

Standing Bear said something Owens didn't understand

to the elder who replied in the same language.

"When you found it, it was just bones. Have you looked at the bones?" Standing Bear asked.

Owens walked over to the smoldering pile of remains. The bones were intact. It would be hard not to see that. They were white and stood out…

"The bones aren't burned," Owens said. "They should be as black as the rest of the debris."

Standing Bear nodded.

"So what do we do to stop it?"

Standing Bear shrugged. "I don't know, but what John Tamanend's ancestors did thousands of years ago stopped it for many lifetimes."

Owens had the remains doused in water to cool them. Then the soldiers gathered up the bones and placed them in the casket. Owens thought about separating the bones, but he wasn't sure if any other material would have been strong enough to hold the creature or weather separating the bones would stop the creature or just lead to multiple creatures being created should this happen again.

While all this was being done, Owens conferred with his superiors about what had happened and what he thought needed to be next.

Two days later, officials approved an alternative plan for the chamber. Construction began four days later. The debris from excavating that chamber was dumped on top of the casket. Every other day, trucks poured cement over the debris pile.

When the new chamber was finished, the old chamber was nearly full of debris. A tunnel wall was constructed and more backfill was added to the gaps behind the wall sealing the casket back inside the mountain.

Over time, the casket and its contents were forgotten.

A buck tread its way over brush and limbs that littered the ground. It kept its head held high. It didn't worry about predators or the fact that it was midday. It just kept moving forward.

It paused over a small hole the size of a gopher hole and lowered its head to sniff at the opening. Its head jerked up as if it sensed something. The brown fur split along the deer's back. It slipped off the deer and seemingly fell into the hole. Then the deer glowed blue and vanished.

OLD KILN ROAD

CHAPTER 1: ANIMAL KILLER

Her own screams woke her from her nap. That's how it always was for Betty Douglas. Sleep was a fleeting thing if it came at all, and it was never a peaceful affair; just something she did to pull herself through to the next day.

But the next day was never any better than the one before it. More of the same emptiness. More of the same fears. More of the same pain.

Betty never left her property anymore because she would have to go past the end of the driveway and that was an evil place. A place where death was stronger than life, and it hurt her to see it. It reminded her of what Old Kiln Road had done to her son... her Peter.

Can an inanimate thing kill?

She had asked herself that question 10,000 times if she had asked it once. Around about the 4,000th time, Betty began to think the answer was "yes."

Old Kiln Road was evil. It was a murderer. In particular, the stretch of road that ran in front of her home. The road ran from Roddy Road north with a couple of hard turns to Motters Station Road. In all, it was about 2.5 miles long with a few dozen homes along it and a lot of open space.

For as long as Betty could remember, there had always been a lot of road kills on Old Kiln Road. Back when Betty used to like to sit on her front porch, she saw a dead animal almost every time she walked out her front door because most of them seemed to be along the stretch of road that ran in front of her property.

Rabbits, dogs, cats, possums, raccoons, and some unidentified remains. Still, she hadn't ever thought it was anything more than the result of a losing battle between Mother Nature and modern technology.

The only thing Betty had thought was odd was how completely the dead animals decayed. She never had to take a shovel out to the road to bury the dead animals because they always seemed to disappear after a few days.

And there was never any smell. Oh, she'd seen the birds

picking over the bones and the flies swarming over the bodies. Then one day she would come out, and the first corpse would have vanished, and a brand new animal lay splattered on the road.

In all her years of porch sitting, Betty had never seen an animal killed, only the remains. Then one overcast day, she saw it happen. Normally, she wouldn't have been outside on such a dreary day, but the house was stifling hot because the air-conditioning needed a shot of freon. Her husband Jack had called the repairman the day before, trying to get him out to the house.

So Betty had walked out onto the porch to get away from the heat. She sat down in her favorite chair, a wooden rocker Jack had bought her when she was pregnant with Peter. As she rocked back and forth, Betty watched the sparse traffic go back and forth on Old Kiln Road, a car every 10 minutes or so, if that much.

She wasn't the only one watching either. On the other side of the two-lane road, a beautiful collie sat in the grass, its head swinging back and forth. The dog had to be someone's pet. Betty wondered where the dog had come from and why it just sat watching the road. It looked as if it was waiting for something.

From the south, an unseen car engine roared as the driver picked up speed on the straight stretch of road. Betty's house was close to one end of that stretch and the only one within a quarter mile.

Peter came to the door and said, "Mom, can I have a cookie?"

Betty looked over her shoulder. Peter was standing in the

doorway, smiling that innocent way he had of grinning. Betty couldn't resist him.

"Only two. And put the jar back when you're done," she said.

Peter went back inside the house, and Betty again turned her attention to the dog on the other side of the road. It was standing now and stretching as if it was preparing to cross the street.

"Don't come now, puppy," Betty muttered to herself. "Can't you hear that car coming?"

The car was maintaining a good clip, probably going about fifty miles an hour. The collie watched it come. Betty was happy that the dog wouldn't become road kill. It was such a pretty dog.

Right before the car passed the dog, it suddenly jumped onto the road. The collie was too close to the car for it to slow down and let it pass. It happened so quickly Betty only had time to open her mouth to yell. The truck hit the dog, knocking it to the ground and then catching the collie under the truck tires. The car slowed, but rather than stop, it sped up to get away from the scene of the accident.

Betty's scream died in her throat as she just stared at the corpse. The dog had committed suicide. That's the only way she could describe it as she looked at the mangled, bloody corpse.

Of course, Jack hadn't believed her. She had told him the whole story when he came home from work that night. He had just muttered, "Stupid mutt" and gone off to watch the evening news. Peter, on the other hand, had asked her if he could have a collie for a pet.

Betty knew it was more than the fact that the dog was stupid. The collie had seen the car coming, and it had jumped in front of the car. That night Betty sat out on the porch staring at the corpse. The first scavengers, the birds, left near sunset, leaving the disfigured corpse laying on the road. By tomorrow morning, other small scavengers would have come and picked over the dead collie.

Even as Betty watched, a raccoon crossed the street and stopped to smell the corpse. While it was chewing on the dead collie's ear, a car along the road and flattened the raccoon. Betty almost screamed.

She had lived in the house for seven years without ever seeing an animal killed on the road, and now she had seen two animals killed within half a day of each other.

She shook her head back and forth. Had the collie moved? No, it was dead. She had seen it killed. But the dog's corpse was moving. It was sinking into the road as if it was a ship sinking in the ocean. How could that be? The asphalt was a solid surface.

Why hadn't she ever noticed this before? No one had ever mentioned something this odd to her, but who actually watched the road? Peter was always playing in the backyard, and Jack was usually away at work. But it had happened. She had seen it. When she had slowed down enough to pay attention to things, she had finally noticed what had been happening right in front of her own home.

That night Betty dreamed of Old Kiln Road as a giant beast. The road was actually a long, black tongue leading into the dark throat of a sleeping beast. The tunnel of trees that shaded the road at the top of the hill formed the throat.

And the beast was always hungry, even in its sleep. It was like an angler fish that dangled its bait to attract food. The road was the bait that lured other animals into the maw of the beast.

CHAPTER 2: THE KILLING ROAD

"Peter, you make sure you stay away from the road," Betty Douglas told her son as they ate breakfast in their kitchen.

He spooned his Corn Pops into his mouth and talked with his mouth full. "I always stay away from the road. You told me this before when I was little," six-year-old Peter said, slightly indignant that his mother still considered him a child.

Betty knew she had told Peter to stay away from the road many times before. It was popular Momtalk. But after seeing what she had seen the day before, Betty felt a need to repeat herself once again. She didn't trust Old Kiln Road. Not the drivers, the road. Something about it was *wrong*. She didn't even like the name. Old Kiln. She always made sure to pronounce the N in Kiln, but too many people let it fade, so it sounded like kill.

Old Kill Road. It lived up to its name.

Betty spent the morning working outside. She painted large yellow signs with black lettering that read: "Slow." When they dried, she nailed the signs on trees at each end of the dangerous stretch of road. She also put up chicken wire along the road to act as a fence to discourage animals from going onto the road. If the animals went around the fence, they would be far enough away from the dangerous portion of the road to make it to the other side.

For two days, Betty sat on the porch and watched how her precautions affected the road. She saw no road kills, and the cars drove slower as they came around the curve. The road seemed to pale from lack of food. At least Betty *hoped* the road paled. She imagined it becoming a light gray during the second day of its fast.

Betty sensed victory close at hand. No longer would the road lure animals to their deaths.

Then she saw Peter's soccer ball bounce over the backyard fence. It rolled to a stop about three feet from the road. As Betty watched, the ball started bouncing again, this time on its own. It bounced up the slight rise to the edge of the road and then across the road. Peter came running from behind the garage, following the ball. He didn't even hesitate as he ran across the road to get the ball.

"Peter!" Betty yelled as she jumped out of the rocking chair.

Her son stopped in the middle of the road at the sound of his mother's voice. As he turned to look at her, a sports car charged around the curve. Betty could tell by the engine noise that it was coming too fast, ignoring her signs.

Peter didn't even have time to scream. The car hit him, and he rolled over the hood, smashing into the windshield head first. The car skidded to a stop, and Peter's body slid forward off the car and fell onto the road, limp as month-old celery.

Betty ran down to the road. Peter lay on the asphalt, a portion of his brain showing through his broken skull. Blood flowed from his body onto the road. The road absorbed the blood like a dry sponge absorbing water... or a thirsty beast drinking greedily. Betty grabbed her son by the shoulders to lift him up, and his head rolled lifelessly backwards. She knew he was dead, but just couldn't believe it.

"Peter! Peter!"

The teenager who had driven the car was standing next to his car with his head buried in his hands as he cried. He slid down the side of the car and sobbed violently, not looking at Betty. Betty held her son in her arms, rocking back and forth until a Thurmont ambulance finally came half an hour later when a passerby saw the accident and phoned it in.

The road turned a darker gray.

Betty sat on the front porch, rocking in her chair and watching the road. In the week since Peter had been killed, the road had fallen back into its rhythm of killing and eating.

Old Kiln Road was a deep ebony now. It was the road that had killed Peter, not the teenage driver of the car. The road had lured Peter onto it so he could be killed. Old Kiln Road was trying to get even with Betty for depriving it of food for two days.

She heard the screen door open on her left, but she didn't look up. She knew who it would be since only two people lived in the house anymore.

Jack set his suitcases down on the porch. "I can send someone else out to Los Angeles. It doesn't have to be me, Bet."

Jack worked as an auditor for a manufacturing company

in Frederick. He usually had a half an hour drive to work, but occasionally, he went on long trips to the firm's corporate offices in Los Angeles.

"I'll be fine. Go," she told him.

"You're not acting fine. I'm worried about you. All you do is sit out here and look at the road where he was killed."

Jack just didn't understand. It wasn't just the spot where Peter had been killed. It was where Peter had been eaten. It was the spot where many animals were eaten day after day. And no one ever noticed. No one but her.

"Please, go, Jack. I'll be fine."

He kissed her on the cheek. "I left all the phone numbers and places where I'll be staying on the bulletin board. If you need me, give me a call, and I'll come right home."

He left and Betty sat on the porch, only seeing him go when he crossed over her field of vision as he drove down Old Kiln Road.

Sometime later, the phone rang. The caller wouldn't be anyone important, so she let it ring until the answering machine picked it up. What was happening out here was more important than anything anyone could say to her.

A small, gray rabbit hopped out into the middle of the road. It sniffed at the asphalt as if he were following a scent across the road. When it reached a certain point in the road, it stopped and lay on its side. A few minutes later, a car came creeping slowly over the hill. Slow enough that the rabbit could have moved in time to get out of the way, but it didn't. It let itself be run over. It committed suicide.

That's what she should do, Betty thought. Life wasn't worth living anymore. Jack still had his work to keep him busy, but her work had been raising Peter, and the road had taken that from her. There was nothing left for her now.

Except to destroy the road. To watch it wither away slowly and agonizingly. To let the road know the pain she felt at the loss of her son. That's what she wanted to do.

Once she made up her mind, Betty knew exactly how she would kill the road. She took Jack's chainsaw out of the garage and walked over the hill. Finding a medium-sized tree near the road, she sawed into it so it toppled across the road, blocking any cars from coming over the hill. Then she walked down the hill and did the same thing to another tree blockading the road. The next thing she did was to take one of the dessert pies from the oven and set in the field to draw the animals away from the road.

Old Kiln Road didn't eat that night, and in the morning it was grayer.

CHAPTER 3: THE ROAD FEEDS

Betty Douglas's plan to kill Old Kiln Road was working. The tree she cut down to block the road kept cars from killing animals that the road tempted onto it. The road turned gray, and things seemed peaceful. Then a Frederick County road crew removed the tree. No accusations were made against Betty, but she was sure they thought she was responsible for blocking the road.

She had to do it because no one believed Old Kiln Road had killed her son, and Betty refused to have her revenge taken from her.

She replaced the "Slow" signs with "Detour" signs to

steer people around the bad stretch of Old Kiln Road. Detour signs wouldn't annoy drivers like the tree had, and the county road crew wouldn't respond as quickly as it had for the tree. Still the cars came, but no animals were killed because Betty kept scaring them away from the road. She couldn't keep her constant patrols up forever, though. She had to stop the cars.

Betty smashed dozens of her empty mason jars at either end of the road. The first few cars that ignored the detour signs were rewarded with flat tires. Traffic stopped and followed the detour.

The next morning, the road was once again a pale gray, starving for food. Betty set more food out in the fields to feed the animals. She checked on her glass traps, but they were gone as if they had never been. Had the road swallowed them, hoping to lure traffic back onto the road?

Betty went into the house and took Jack's hunting rifle down from above the mantle. She knew how to use it because Jack had taken her deer hunting with him a few times during hunting season when he couldn't find any friends to go with him. Betty loaded the Remington and went out to the road for her patrols.

About 25 yards from the road, she saw a pickup truck ignore the detour sign and head up Old Kiln Road. She raised the rifle to her shoulder, took aim, and fired just the way Jack had taught her. She shot the truck tires out, then ran off before the driver got out of the car. She walked to the other end of the road and waited. Soon enough, someone else ignored the detour sign. Betty put two holes in his radiator, stopping him from going any further.

The road went hungry another day.

The next day another pickup truck tried to ignore the detour sign and lost two tires. Old Kiln Road went hungry for a fourth day.

On the morning of the fifth day, Betty went out to the porch and wasn't surprised to see the asphalt had dried out. It looked rough, like a patch of dried skin. Cracks ran through, making it look like a sun-baked river bed.

She patrolled the road with the rifle and was satisfied to see all the cars obeying the detour sign. However, police had barricaded the road and officers patrolled the roads and surrounding woods. One officer questioned her, and Betty played innocent about what was going on.

How long would it be before the police opened the road? Would it be long enough for the road to be destroyed?

As the sun set that night, Betty watched the asphalt finally crumble into dust exposing the gravel road bed. But there was something else among the gravel. Bones. Lots of them. Probably the bones of every animal that had even been killed on that stretch of road. The small skeletons gleamed brightly in the fading light. Betty had starved the road to death and won.

How many animals had died to feed the road? How many people like her Peter had been killed?

She walked to the edge of the road and kicked at the gravel to loosen it like a hunter kicks at his fallen prey to make sure it's dead.

"I don't know what made you so bloodthirsty, but I hope whatever it was rots with you in hell," Betty said.

She moved to kick it again, but as she did, Old Kiln Road

decayed just a bit more. The edge of the roadway collapsed under her foot. Betty yelled as she lost her balance and fell onto the gravel. She put out her hands to break her fall, but the rifle got caught in between her and the road. It went off, and Betty shot herself in the stomach.

She fell onto the road, not dead but dying. She screamed for help, but no one was nearby to come to her aid. All the drivers were too afraid to travel this stretch of Old Kiln Road, and Jack was in Los Angeles. She was alone.

Her blood pumped through the hole in her stomach, down her side, and onto the road. As it touched the roadway, it immediately turned black restoring the asphalt. The changes spread like a ripple on water, restoring the road even as Betty lay on top of it dying.

Would the police find her body and think she was a victim of the sniper they were searching for?

Betty wasn't going to let the road take her body. She would not be like the collie that she had seen commit suicide.

Holding one hand against the bloody hole in her stomach, Betty tried to rise up on her knees so she could crawl away. She moved one leg forward, but it was a struggle. Her leg had sunk into the asphalt and it only pulled free with a loud sucking sound.

She grabbed with her free hand for the fence she had built alongside the road to keep the animals away. Her hand closed around one of the wooden posts, but the wooden post snapped off in her hand. She fell forward on her face and the road sucked her back a few inches.

Betty rolled onto her back and fired the rifle into the road. Again and again she fired until the rifle clicked empty. The bullets didn't even leave a mark on the road. They simply disappeared into the soft asphalt. She beat on the road with the rifle until she was too weak to pull the rifle free from the road.

The road pulled her a few inches closer. She was now sitting in the roadway.

How do you kill something that is not alive?

Betty realized she couldn't win, but it made her feel good to resist the evil of the road. With her remaining strength, she lunged out of the roadway so that her upper body fell onto the grass.

Let her blood nourish the ground, not the road. She wouldn't help the road live.

Once Old Kiln Road restored itself to its original condition, Betty knew she had lost. After all her efforts, the road had finally found its meal. She felt herself pulled onto the road and sinking into the surface as if she wasn't laying on hard asphalt but thick, black tar. She sunk a few inches into the asphalt thinking she would stop when she touched the hard ground. But she kept sinking deeper and deeper. As the soft asphalt filled her ears, Betty tried to raise her head to keep it above the surface. She had to stop soon. This is what happened to the road kills that laid on the road for days at a time. Almost like the La Brea Tar Pits.

The road covered Betty's face.

Jack turned onto Old Kiln Road. It had been a quiet ride home. Not unusual, but the newspaper he picked up at the airport had said there had been a sniper shooting at cars along the road. From the description given, it sounded like it had been close to his house.

As he came over the last rise before his driveway, a chipmunk ran out into the road so fast that Jack couldn't swerve to avoid it. He hit it with his right front tire and killed it.

Stupid animal. Didn't they know better than to stay away from the road?

FIRE, FIRE

CHAPTER 1: MASTER OF THE FLAMES

Meshach Hunt stood on the mound of earth until his boots began smoking. Then he danced around yelling, "Ouch, ouch, ouch!"

Fifteen feet below him, his brother Abednego grinned, but he said, "Stop fooling around, Shack. We've got more logs to stack on the number three pile."

Meshach was only a year younger than Abednego, but he might as well have been 20 years younger. He acted like jumping the stacks was a game of hot foot. They both knew stepping too hard in the wrong spot might lead to a hole that swallowed the collier up and dropped him into the fires smoldering beneath. Meshach saw it as a challenge. Abednego saw it as a danger.

Meshach stopped his jumping. He shifted the dirt on the mound with his shovel, covering the smoke hole. It was important to keep the air out and the heat in the mound. It controlled the burning going on beneath the mound. In another week, this mound would be a load of charcoal for Catoctin Furnace at the base of the mountain.

The furnace had been operating for decades, creating pig iron for stoves, utensils, and other things. The stone and brick stack was ever hungry, consuming 800 bushels of charcoal each day. Abednego wasn't so good with his numbers, but a foreman at the furnace told him that to get that much charcoal, the woodcutters felled an acre of hardwood trees each day. They brought the trees to colliers like the Hunt brothers, who turned the wood into charcoal.

Meshach finished his inspection of the mound while Abednego walked over to the pile of logs the woodcutters had finished delivering a few minutes ago. The number three stack would be ready to start burning tomorrow. This was the last load of logs needed.

Meshach and Abednego had spent two days preparing this mound. In the very center was a fagan, a pole around which the logs were stacked, and once removed, the hole left behind would create the chimney in the stack. Although the stack was already started, Abednego needed Meshach's help setting the logs onto the stack.

Meshach finally climbed off the stack and down the

ladder. He walked over to his brother, and the pair carried the oak logs to the stack and then tilted them onto the other logs that formed the circular, cone-like structure. Then they stepped back to look at the result of three days' work.

The brothers had stacked 40 cords of 12-foot-long logs in expanding circles around a chimney flue. The chimney had already been stuffed with sticks and other kindling. Now, the colliers' job would be to fill in the gaps between the logs with sticks. Then they would cover it all with a layer of dirt.

Once that was done, they would remove the fagan, and the brothers would drop embers into the chimney to get a fire started in the center of the stack of logs. Then they would let the logs slowly burn for two weeks. The dirt covering kept the air out so that they could control the burn rate.

After two weeks, they would open what remained of the stacks and spread out to cool like the number four stack was doing.

Seen from a distance, someone might have thought the collection of a dozen structures with smoke rolling from their tops was a small village. However, this village only had two residents. It was enough for Abednego. It had always been him and his brother since they were children. They didn't need anyone else.

Abednego wiped off his sweat with the back of his arm. "Just in time for lunch," he said.

Neither brother was married, although they were in their thirties. Abednego didn't blame the women. He rarely saw them. Who would want to live in a shack on Catoctin Mountain? The only people the Hunt brothers saw regularly were colliers, woodcutters, and furnace workers.

They walked into their hut, which was a windowless room that resembled the stacks except it had a doorway on the side.

They rinsed their hands in a bucket of water and ate bread, cheese, and apples for lunch. It wasn't fancy, but it filled them up. They ate little hot food. Neither of them wanted to cook over a fire after tending stacks all day. They lived with a perpetual sheen of sweat even in the winter.

Besides, they didn't want to eat too much. No one wanted to feel heavy walking on a charcoal stack.

After lunch, the brothers raked the soil off number two stack to get at the cooled charcoal underneath. They shoveled the charcoal into the wagon bed, filling it up. Then they tied a tarp over it. The trip down the mountain could be bouncy, and Abednego didn't want to lose half his load before he reached the furnace.

When everything was loaded, Abednego climbed up into the seat.

"Want to come along, Shack?" he asked.

Meshach shook his head. "No, I'll take care of things here, Ben."

Abednego nodded, not surprised. His brother never made the journey to Catoctin Furnace. He was content to stay on the mountain and watch over the stacks. Abednego lived for the trips off the mountain to drop off coal at the furnace. It gave him an excuse to go into town and talk to people, especially women.

Of course, he understood Meshach's position. Those fires burned for two to three weeks at a time, and someone needed to watch them to make sure they didn't get too hot or go out.

It just didn't need to be Meshach who always did it. He seemed to sense how much Abednego looked forward to the trips off the mountain.

When Abednego reached the Frederick Road between Mechanicstown and Catoctin Furnace, he turned south. He smiled at a woman he saw hanging laundry on a line. He might have stopped to talk, but it was obvious from the laundry that she probably had a husband. Besides, Abednego knew he didn't present well. He was covered in soot, as always, and smelled like wood smoke.

The furnace that gave the village of Catoctin Furnace its name was 32-feet tall, an impressive site amid all the nearby one-story buildings. A water wheel, mill pond, and races, a coal house to store charcoal, the bridge and bridge house to charge the stack, and a cast house were all nearby structures supporting the furnace operation.

Further away were the homes for the workmen, which had their own buildings that supported them; stores, barns, stables, and a church. Catoctin Furnace had hundreds of workers. Miners dug the iron from the ground. Lumberers felled the trees and colliers prepared the charcoal from them. Fillers charged the furnace. Founders smelted the iron and cast it. And all of these people lived near the furnace, except for the colliers.

They stayed on the mountain with the stacks that had to be watched around the clock, even on Sundays. However, some colliers did work in shifts, so they could live at least part of the time in town. It was just easier for the Hunts to live near their stacks. They were used to living by themselves. It seemed like they always had.

Abednego unloaded the charcoal into the coal house and then walked over to watch the men working the furnace. He could feel the heat from the fires burning the furnace 100 feet away.

He watched a pair of shirtless, sweaty men shovel charcoal into the fire to keep the flames burning hot enough to melt the iron ore, which was also in the furnace. This was the opposite of Abednego's job, which was to control the fire and create a smoldering heat.

He stared into the tall, dancing flames, entranced by their undulations. He rarely saw the flames he worked with, and if he did, it was usually a bad thing. These flames devoured the charcoal, while Abednego's flames savored the wood.

He reached a hand toward the flames and imagined holding it in his hand. He had held a burning coal in his hand for a short time once. It had seemed like a living thing as the light from the ember pulsed. It reminded him of a firefly. Then it had grown too hot, and he had tossed it away.

He controlled the fire. He commanded it to do his bidding, and it did. He was the master of the flames.

CHAPTER 2: A DEATH IN THE FAMILY

After dropping off a load of charcoal at the coal house in Catoctin Furnace, Abednego Hunt walked down Frederick Road to the nearby store for supplies. He and his brother, Meshach, had a small garden at their collier's camp on Catoctin Mountain. It provided fresh vegetables, but the brothers still needed staples like coffee, flour, and sugar from time to time.

Abednego looked over the offerings on the shelves, but he was really watching Nellie Latimer behind the counter. She was 22 years old and already a widow. Her husband had been a woodcutter. He had died last year when a tree fell the wrong way and crushed him. Now, Nellie worked for her father who owned the store.

Abednego liked to watch her move and listen to her laugh. She was smart, too, which didn't say much, since Abednego never finished school. He had had to go to work after his parents died from a fever.

"Can I help you find something, Ben?" Nellie asked.

"I'm just looking everything over," Abednego said.

"It doesn't change that much between your visits, and it's not that interesting."

"That may be, but I'm used to seeing trees and flames, so anything different is worth taking time to look over." Abednego walked over to stand closer. "How have you been?"

"All right, I suppose. My father works me harder than his other clerk," Nellie said.

"You could always get another job."

"I could get other work, but it wouldn't pay as much. It pays to be the boss's daughter sometimes."

She smiled at him. Her teeth were white. Abednego pressed his lips together. He doubted his teeth were that white. He rarely brushed them. Just didn't seem to be that much cause being so isolated on the mountain.

"So what can I get you?" she asked.

"Do you have any newspapers?" Abednego liked to read when he had time. He tried to keep on top of what was happening.

Nellie looked under the counter. "I've got four from Frederick, one from Gettysburg, and one from Hagerstown."

"I'll take the most-recent one."

She laid a copy of the Frederick Herald on the counter. It was three days old.

"Anything else?"

Abednego bought coffee and sugar, and he took a risk that a dozen eggs could make it back up to his hut on the mountain without cracking. He eyed his purchases, comparing the cost against how much money he had with him.

"Add a nickel's worth of candy to the order, Nellie," Abednego said. "I'll bring Shack a treat since he never comes off the mountain."

"Who's that?"

"Shack. Meshach, my brother."

"Oh." She raised an eyebrow, but said nothing more.

Nellie tallied up the order and placed the items in a bag. Abednego paid the bill and headed back out to the wagon which he had left near the furnace.

He walked past the furnace to the ironmaster's house. It was a large three-story home built of stone and wood. It had 18 rooms inside. It could probably contain all the stacks that Abednego and Meshach managed with room left over. How large was the ironmaster's family for him to need such a large home? Abednego and Meshach lived in a single room with no windows. If they had lived in a place like the ironmaster's house, they might go for days without seeing each other.

He did have to admit it was a beautiful home with its

wide porches and boxwoods surrounding it. It probably had large beds with thick feather mattresses. How wonderful it must be to sleep on a cloud at night.

Abednego walked back and climbed into his wagon. He looked up at Catoctin Mountain. It looked like a dog with mange. There were still plenty of trees, but he could also see bare patches where the woodcutters had cleared everything away. Other areas showed newer growth where tree had been replanted. They weren't old enough to harvest yet, but the woodcutters would eventually come back to them. The furnace was a ravenous beast that demanded to be fed. Colliers like the Hunt brothers brought in wagon loads of charcoal each day to keep the fires burning. The charcoal was the first layer put down in the furnace. Then came limestone and finally the iron ore. Then the layers repeated until the furnace was filled to the top. It all started with the charcoal.

He drove the horse north toward Mechanicstown and turned west to head up the mountain. The dirt road wound back and forth, making its way ever higher. The ride got rougher when he left the main road to head to where their camp was. It was fortunate he didn't have to pull big loads uphill. He would have needed another horse.

He drove through stands of trees that were probably 10 to 15 years old. In another five years, the woodcutters might be felling them again. Who knows where their camp would be then? They moved it twice a year to stay close to woodcutters since they had to use mule-drawn sleds to bring the logs to the colliers. The closer the collier camps were to the trees, the less time was wasted hauling logs.

As Abednego approached the camp, he saw Meschach

jumping the stack on number one. He shouldn't be on that stack. It was too close to finishing. It was already starting to shrink as the logs burned down to charcoal.

"Hi, Ben!" Meshach called, waving.

"I bought you some candy!" Abednego said.

Meschach grinned. A gust of wind blew through the clearing. The wind swirled and blew leaves onto the stack. They floated upward on the small tendril of smoke from the chimney.

Then Meshach disappeared.

Abednego blinked and stared at the top of the stack. Then he saw the larger hole near the chimney, and he heard his brother scream.

Abednego dropped the reins and scrambled up the ladder onto the stack.

"Shack!"

Released from the confines of the stack, more smoke rolled out and the flames in the hearth ignited.

Meshach screamed again.

As Abednego stepped up to the hole, the edge collapsed. He fell backwards rather into the hole as his brother had done. He rolled off the stack and landed hard on the ground. His breath left him in a gasp.

Meshach screamed, "Ben, help me!"

Abednego rolled to his feet and climbed back onto the stack. This time, he lay on his stomach and looked into the hole. He couldn't see anything. The hole was dark and smoke poured out making it hard to keep his eyes open.

Meschach continued screaming. Abednego reached into the hole.

"Shack, grab my hand! Grab it! I'll pull you out!"

That was going to be the only way to get his brother out quickly. He felt something slap his hand, but it moved away quickly.

"That was my hand, Shack! Grab it!"

Meschach stopped screaming.

"Shack! Shack! Shack!"

Meshach never answered.

CHAPTER 3: ALL THAT REMAINS

Abednego Hunt rolled onto his backside and slid off the smoldering log stack. His younger brother, Meshach, had stepped on a weak spot and fallen into the center of the stack where the fires were slowly turning the logs into charcoal for the Catoctin Iron furnace.

He rolled off the edge of the stack and hit the ground hard. He quickly scrambled to his feet and looked for a shovel. He grabbed it and scraped at the layer of earth that covered the log stack and held in the heat.

Abednego exposed a log and clawed at with his fingers, but he couldn't get a grip. He pried at a log with the shovel, trying to work it loose. The log wiggled, and he drove it deeper into the gap until he could get a grip on it. He pulled until he could roll the log to the side.

Once the log was out of the way and there was a gap in the stack, it was easier to get at the other logs.

Abednego peered into the interior of the stack. "Shack! Shack, answer me!"

His brother said nothing.

Abednego scrambled to pull another log free. Then he reached into the stack. "Grab my hand! Grab my hand!"

Nothing happened.

He crawled into the stack, ignoring the heat and pain from the burning embers. Flames flared up as more air reached the embers.

He pulled another log free. He needed more light inside the stack so that he could see where his brother was. The third log he pulled free fell into the stack, sending a cloud of embers into the air. They stung where they touched Abednego's flesh and smoldered on his clothing.

Abednego still couldn't see Meshach. He kept pulling at logs, hoping that the next one would somehow reveal his brother. He pulled so many free that the stack finally collapsed. One log hit Abednego on the shoulder and sent him sprawling into the center of the stack.

He no longer felt any pain or even noticed that his shirt was smoking. He stood up and looked around, but he didn't see his brother. All he saw was ashes.

It couldn't be. His brother had fallen into the stack only a few minutes ago. There should be a body or bones, at the very least.

Tears streamed down his cheeks. "Shack!"

No one answered.

Abednego walked into the cabin he shared with his brother and found a box filled with canned goods. He took the cans out and walked back out to the flattened charcoal stack.

He stared at the ashes. Some of them had to be his brother, but he couldn't tell the difference between any of them.

They were all gray.

Abednego filled the box with the ashes he thought might be Meshach. They were the ones near the center where Shack had fallen into the stack. He tried to feel a connection to the ashes. He felt like he should be able to feel a connection if the ashes were Shack's, but he felt nothing. He put his fingers in the ashes and slowly stirred them.

Why couldn't he sense his brother?

Abednego drove the wagon off the mountain and into Catoctin Furnace. It felt unusual coming down the mountain in a wagon not weighed down by charcoal, especially since he had been here yesterday. The box filled with Meshach's ashes sat on the bench seat next to him.

He drove to the small stone church John O'Brien, an owner of the furnace, had built last year in honor of his wife.

Abednego walked inside, cradling the box in his arms. The church was empty. He was about to leave when Rev. John Clark Hoyle walked in from the other end.

"May I help you?" the reverend asked.

"Reverend, I need you to hold a service for my brother," Abednego said.

The reverend motioned for Abednego to sit in a pew.

"Tell me what happened," Rev. Hoyle asked.

Abednego teared up. "He burned in a fire yesterday. I couldn't get to him in time."

Rev. Hoyle put a hand on Abednego's shoulder. "That's terrible, son. I'm so sorry for your loss."

Abednego wiped at his eyes. "I'd like to bury him in the cemetery, Reverend, and have you say some words over him."

"Certainly. Is the body with the undertaker?"

Abednego patted the box in his lap. "No, this is all that's left of him."

Rev. Hoyle's eyes widened. "But that box isn't big enough…"

"It's all that was left."

Rev. Hoyle shook his head. "No, there would be bones. Maybe you were mistaken."

"I saw him fall into the stack. I heard him scream."

"But the charcoal stacks don't burn hot enough to leave nothing but ash." Rev. Hoyle lifted the lid on the box and stared at what was inside. "This is nothing but ash. You can even see the charcoal bits in it."

Abednego slapped the lid closed. "That's all that remains of my brother. I was there. I should know."

Rev. Hoyle pressed his lips together and was silent as he stared at Abednego. Finally, he said, "I believe you are sincere, young man. I don't know what happened with your brother, but that is not a body. I have seen burned bodies before. That is not one."

"I'm telling you it is."

Rev. Hoyle shook his head. "I'm sorry. I don't want to add to your grief."

Abednego picked up the box and walked out of the church. He didn't know what to say, but he felt anything he said to the reverend would be unkind. Abednego would just have to bury the body himself.

He climbed into the wagon and put the box on the seat next to him. He drove the wagon to the superintendent's office. The Superintendent Pitzer was sitting at his desk when Abednego knocked on the door. The superintendent waved him inside.

"Can I help you?" the burly superintendent asked.

"I'm Abednego Hunt. I'm one of the colliers. I work with my brother, Meshach." Abednego sat down in the chair in front of the Superintendent Pitzer's desk. "Well, the thing is, there was an accident yesterday, and my brother fell into the stack and burned to death."

The superintendent's eyes narrowed, and he lifted his chin. "I hadn't heard anything."

"No, sir, that's why I'm here. I came to arrange for my brother's burial and to collect his death benefit."

"I see."

The superintendent stood and walked over to a bookshelf. He carried a book back to the desk. He opened the book and started leafing through the pages. Then he ran his finger down a list of names.

"I see your name, Abednego, but I don't see your brother's," Pitzer said.

"What does that mean?"

"It means he is not employed by the furnace, and you are not owed any death benefit."

"But Meschach's been working here as long as I have."

"Our records say otherwise."

"You're trying to cheat me!"

"I would not cheat anyone of a death benefit. I don't want to add to a family's grief, but your brother was not employed here. I see your name, but I can find no record of a Meshach Hunt working here or ever being paid wages. I'm sorry."

Abednego stood up. "This just isn't right."

"Unless you can show me something that proves he worked for us and was paid, I can't do anything."

Abednego shook his head. "No, it just isn't right."

He turned and walked out of the office. He kept his clenched fists at his side. Why were people treating him and Meshach like this? Didn't they have any compassion? Did they hate him so much? What had he done to offend them?

He climbed into the wagon and head back toward Mechanicstown. He had a funeral to plan.

CHAPTER 4: THE FIRE WILL JUDGE

Abednego Hunt stood facing the wooden cross he had carved. He knew you were supposed to wear your Sunday best for funerals, but he only had two sets of clothes, and they were both work clothes. He had carefully washed one set, though, so he could properly say goodbye to his brother Meshach.

He held a box of Meshach's ashes. It wasn't a big box, and he wasn't even sure whether it held Shack's ashes. This had been all he could find after his brother fell into the burning charcoal stack yesterday.

Since Rev. Hoyle at the church in town had refused to bury the ashes, Abednego buried them here on Catoctin Mountain, near the charcoal stacks where he and Meshach had lived and worked.

He dug a hole in the ground about two feet deep and placed the box of ashes in it. Then he recited a few Bible verses he remembered from childhood. They didn't pertain to death or burials, but they were only things Abednego knew.

He buried the box and stood crying over the grave. He already missed his brother.

That evening, as he lay in his cot in the ramshackle cabin he and Meshach called home, Abednego imagined his brother lying on his cot talking to him.

"It wasn't your fault, Ben," Shack said.

"I know, but I miss you all the same," Abednego told him.

"It was the iron company. They don't care about us. They wouldn't pay you my death benefit."

"They said you weren't on the payroll."

"I was, though. You know that. You know I drew pay."

Abednego nodded, "I know, but they won't listen."

"Then the fire will judge them."

That startled Abednego, and he sat up, wide awake. He walked outside. Some of the charcoal stacks still smoldered, but he had done nothing to tend them since Shack had died. Let them burn down to nothing for all he cared.

He walked over to a stack that had collapsed. He could see the glowing embers of what remained of the fire and logs mixed in with the dirt that had covered the stacks. Abednego should have been shoveling the charcoal into the wagon.

Instead, he kicked at the dirt, exposing the charcoal and remaining embers. He picked up one orange glowing piece of wood, not even feeling pain. He threw it at the shack. It hit the wall and fell to the ground.

He picked up another ember and threw it. This one landed on the roof of the shack and began smoking. He threw another and another. He felt no pain, although his hands were red. What he felt was relief.

Little wisps of flame appeared on the roof where the embers had taken hold. He stood and watched as the flames grew. He didn't worry. He owned little and wouldn't miss any of it.

He walked back into the shack and felt the heat from the surrounding flames. He looked up at the yellow flames spreading along the roof.

He closed his eyes and held his arms out to his side. *The fire will judge them.*

Abednego heard timbers hit the ground as the fire ate through them and weakened the structure. He kept his eyes closed and waited. The heat grew intense and the flames loud. He couldn't hear anything except for the cracking of wood and whoosh of flames growing. They whispered to him, but he couldn't understand what they said. They must be passing their judgement upon him.

He waited, wincing finally at the heat.

Occasionally, a flame licked at his body, but he kept his eyes closed and waited.

Then there were a final great whoosh and crash. He felt a gust of wind. Then he felt cool air, at least cooler air.

He opened his eyes.

The shack had collapsed around him, but it had fallen in such a way that no burning pieces of wood had hit him. They lay around him, some of them still burning.

The fire had judged him, but had it rejected him or found him worthy?

Did it matter? It was time for it to judge the others who had turned their backs on the Hunt brothers, especially Meshach.

Abednego rode the horse down the mountain in the dark. It

was surefooted, and he let it find its way with little guidance.

The streets were deserted. The workers started early in the morning. They needed their sleep.

He rode into Catoctin Furnace and tied the horse to a tree. Then he walked into town and past the furnace. He stood looking at the ironmaster's house. All the lamps had been extinguished for the night, and the windows were dark.

He walked closer, being careful not to raise any noise. He circled the house and found the woodshed. He spent the next hour hauling the logs from the shed and spreading them around the base of the house. Although the house was primarily stone, it had plenty of wooden siding and beams. He added kindling and stood back to admire his work.

It would burn, but not quickly.

He hurried back out to the furnace and filled a bucket with lamp oil. He carried it back to the house and splashed it on the walls and wood he had piled around the base. He made two more trips and repeated the process.

When he finished his preparations, Abednego used his flints to start a fire on each side of the house. Then he moved into the woods. He watched the flames grow and spread. When it grew brighter, he moved back deeper into the shadows.

The flames had taken hold well before he heard the first cry raised. The yells quickly rose in number, and he began seeing shadows as people rushed to find the water barrels. He had tipped the ones closest to the house over. The fire crew brought the pump wagon over to the house and a bucket brigade formed to fill the wagon's tank.

Abednego sat down and watched the fire burn. The

flames reached high into the sky. He watched as some people attempted to carry out valuables from the house. They knew it was a lost cause.

A woman wailed loudly, probably the ironmaster's wife.

Abednego sighed with satisfaction. Then he walked to where he tied the horse and rode it back up the mountain, where he made himself a bed under a pine tree and slept.

CHAPTER 5: INVESTIGATION

Paul Cresap woke with his head throbbing and someone pounding on the door. He tried to open his eyes, but they were crusted over. He rubbed his eyelashes to break up the crust. Even then, he would have preferred to keep his eyes closed.

Someone knocked on the door to office again. "Sheriff! Sheriff!"

Paul sat up. "Wait a minute! I need to dress."

He stood up slowly and pulled his suspenders over his shoulders. He walked out of the single cell that Mechanicstown had. Since it also served as Paul's bedroom more often than not, it meant he had little incentive to arrest anyone. He didn't want to lose his bedroom.

He walked out of the cell and across the office. He opened the door and saw Tom Weller. He owned a dry goods store on Church Street. Paul often bought his coffee beans there.

"Sheriff, there's been another fire," Tom said. He was out of breath, and Paul guessed he had run from his home above his store.

"Another fire?"

"Didn't you hear the fire bell ringing earlier?"

Paul shook his head. He wasn't about to tell Tom that he had been passed out drunk and wouldn't have heard a black powder explosion if it had gone off under his bed.

Paul said, "Apparently not. Besides, fires aren't my jurisdiction."

It turned out two of the fires hadn't even been in Mechanicstown. The ironmaster's home in Catoctin Furnace had burned earlier this evening. Then Rev. John Clark Hoyle's home had burned down sometime. That house had been on Frederick Road, not far from the church he presided over in Catoctin Furnace.

Someone had told Paul about both of them, but he hadn't done anything because they were outside of the town limits.

"But three fires!" Tom said. "That can't be coincidence. Something needs to be done."

Even in his drunken state, Paul realized Tom was probably right. Mechanicstown might have a fire a month, usually from sparks escaping a fireplace, but three in one night? It probably wasn't accidental.

"Where is this fire?" Paul asked.

"It's the Worthy place on Water Street."

That home was in Mechanicstown. The people in town would expect Paul to check it out. "Is the fire out?" Paul asked.

Tom nodded. "Just about."

First, the ironmaster's mansion, then the reverend's home on Frederick Street, and now a house on Water Street.

"Who owns the Worthy Place?" Paul asked.

"Jonah Worthy. He owns the general store in Catoctin Furnace," Tom told him.

It was like someone was making his way from the furnace and up the mountain. Paul also realized that for three fires to burn in one night, they had to be started fairly quickly. Each fire would divert people to it. There probably hadn't been too many people left to form the bucket brigade at Jonah Worthy's house. People might still be at the fire on Frederick Road.

"I'll go out the Worthy place shortly," Paul said.

He went back into his office and picked up the bucket. He walked out back to fill it with water from the pump and relieve himself in the outhouse. Then he walked back inside to wash himself off and dress. He combed his hair to make himself look presentable.

Then he saddled his horse and rode out to the West Main Street. Then he turned south on Water Street. The Worthy place was just a shell of blackened timbers by the time Paul reached it. It was still smoking. He saw the Worthys rummaging through the remains, seeing if there was anything they could salvage. He wished them luck and hoped they would find something to help them rebuild their lives.

Paul hadn't been so lucky. He had lost his family and his farm. Of course, it hadn't been a fire that took them away. He'd been too drunk most of the time to run his farm, and he had fallen behind on the taxes. The county took the farm, and then his wife and daughter left him to go live with her parents.

It surprised him that the townspeople elected him sheriff. Paul had run because he needed the work. He was lucky no one else wanted the job, or he would still be looking for work.

Paul walked over to Jonah Worthy, who stopped what he was doing.

"Did everyone get out all right, Jonah?"

Jonah Worthy looked like he had been in a fight. His clothing was torn. His face was covered in dirt, and he looked despondent. "Mary was just getting up to start the morning fires in the stove when she saw the flames."

"Where did it start?"

"That just it, Sheriff. She said the flames were all around the house. They worked their way in. We gathered the children and used blankets to get through the fires at the back door."

Paul patted the older man on the shoulder. Then he walked around the edge of the house. He could see pieces of logs all around the perimeter. These weren't boards, but logs the size of firewood.

He scratched at his beard and considered what he was seeing. He didn't like it. He didn't like it at all.

He mounted his horse and rode his horse further south to Rev. Hoyle's house on Frederick Road. It looked much the same as the Worthy house, although the fire hadn't destroyed it entirely because the house had been constructed of stone. The walls were standing, but the roof had collapsed.

Paul walked to the edge of the house and saw pieces of logs all along the sides where there shouldn't be wood.

He suspected he was dealing with an arsonist, but why would someone even try to burn a stone building down. Certainly he had damaged it, but the reverend could gut the interior and rebuilt the roof. It wasn't a total loss like the Worthy house, which is what Paul would have thought an arsonist would have wanted.

So, if complete destruction wasn't the goal, what was? Did the arsonist know the people who lived in the houses? This house belonged to the reverend at Harriet Church. Jonah Worthy owned the store in Catoctin Furnace, and the iron company owned the ironmaster's mansion.

Paul nodded slowly. So, all three owners had connections to the iron company, but was that enough of a connection? He could understand someone being angry with the iron company, and maybe even the owner of the store, but a reverend? Paul had met Rev. Hoyle. He was as nice as they came.

Honestly, it surprised Paul there weren't more fires at the furnace. They kept the fires hot enough to turn iron into liquid. Imagine what damage it could do if some that molten iron was thrown on a house? This all looked like was it was the work of a well-set wood fire, though.

Paul suspected this was the work of an arsonist because the two houses he had seen had been burned from all around the outside inward, and he suspected he would find the same thing at the ironmaster's mansion. Paul was in over his head. He was just a farmer, and a drunk one at that.

CHAPTER 6: HOT ON THE TRAIL

Rubbing his eyes and yawning, Mechanicstown Sheriff Paul Cresap rode his horse into the collier's camp on Catoctin Mountain. This was the fourth camp he had visited today. The colliers moved their camps from time to time to stay close to lumber being cut for the Catoctin Furnace. The furnace needed 800 bushels of charcoal each day to run, and each pound of charcoal came from an acre of hardwood trees.

A couple of people in the village of Catoctin Furnace had told Paul they had heard something about a collier burning to death. Paul thought it might be a fourth arson fire, particularly if the arsonist who had burned homes in Catoctin Furnace, along Frederick Road, and on West Main Street in Mechanicstown had been setting fires as he moved west. It would make sense that there was a fire on the mountain. It was a lucky thing the arsonist hadn't started a forest fire.

Paul had had little luck finding out who had burned to death, and he was beginning to think it was just a story. The colliers at each camp would tell him no one in their group had died, and then they would direct him to another camp.

Paul knew something was off about this camp as soon as he rode in. The other camps had been a collection of smoking mounds of earth or circles of charcoal that needed to be raked from the dirt. The colliers tended to sing, swear, or just cough from the wood smoke.

This camp had mounds, but only a couple were smoking. A couple of others had collapsed but hadn't been raked out. Paul also saw what looked like had been a cabin that had been burned to the ground.

And the place was quiet. If not for the wood smoke, he would have said it was abandoned.

"Hello," Paul called.

A man walked out from behind one stack. Soot covered most of his exposed skin.

115

"Who are you?"

"Sheriff Cresap from Mechanicstown."

"This isn't Mechanicstown."

"No, but I heard that someone had been burned to death up here. Do you know anything about it?"

The man nodded. "It was my brother."

"And who are you?"

"Abednego Long."

"Can you tell me what happened? It may tie into some other things that have happened," Paul asked.

"Meshach — that's my brother — was on top of a stack, and it opened up under him. He fell through and burned. I couldn't get to him in time." Abednego shook his head. "It was horrible. The screams…"

Paul stared at the stacks. They looked like mounds of earth to him. He had seen them as the colliers built them in other camps, though. He knew there was a stack of logs beneath the earth. The dirt was used to control the amount of air that got into the stacks.

"It was an accident, then?" Paul asked.

"Of course it was. Meshach didn't jump into the center of a burning stack on purpose!"

Paul held up a hand. "Sorry. That's not what I meant. I mean, no one could have done anything to the stack to make it give way under your brother."

Abednego thought for a moment and shook his head. "No. It's not the first time something like that has happened. It all depends on how the logs burn." He paused. "Why would you think someone did it to Shack on purpose?"

"I don't, but someone set fires last night at the furnace

and in my town. They are all connected. I thought the fire that killed your brother might be, too."

"What makes you think those fires are connected?"

"They happened on the same night, and they didn't start naturally. Whoever tried to burn the houses down, set them all up the same way."

"Nothing like that happened here. This was an accident I wished never happened."

Paul nodded. "Sorry for your loss."

He looked at the ground and picked up a piece of wood that had been turned into charcoal. Then he looked over at the charred beams of what had been a cabin. They both were burned wood, but the charcoal was darker and denser. It had to be burned in a special way to become charcoal. It didn't come from a regular fire.

"This is charcoal, isn't it?" Paul asked, holding up the chunk he had picked up.

"That's what we… I make here."

"What's the difference between this and burned wood?"

"That is burned wood. We just burn it in a certain way, so it will continue to burn and burn hotter than wood. It can't have too much air when it burns, or it won't be of any use as charcoal, but if it has too little air, it won't burn fully."

Paul nodded and walked back to his horse. Abednego followed him.

"What are you going to do now?" the collier asked.

"I've got some thinking to do and an arsonist to catch."

Paul headed back to his office. When he got there, he took his bottle from his desk drawer and poured himself a drink. He could concentrate better when the whiskey took the edge off the day.

He pulled the piece of charcoal out and set it on the desk in front of him. He had found charcoal around each of the houses that had been burned. It couldn't have been left over from the fire, according to Abednego. Also, while it wouldn't have been unusual to find it at the ironmaster's house, it would have been odd to find it at the other two houses. People around here used firewood in their stoves. It was abundant and cheaper than charcoal.

It would have required a lot of charcoal to build a fire around three houses if it was used for that. Whoever had started the fires had access to a lot of charcoal and knew how to use it.

Then there was how the logs that were used in the fire were laid upright against the houses rather than being piled in one spot or lengthwise along the houses. Colliers stacked wood that way and also had access to charcoal.

Things were pointing to a collier as the arsonist, but there were a couple dozen of them on the mountain. Which one would have wanted to start the fires and why?

Paul fell asleep trying to figure this out.

He woke up coughing. He sat up and quickly doubled over as his coughing continued. He opened his eyes, but they watered. When he finally opened his eyes, he saw smoke filling the room.

He ran to the door. He reached out to open it, but when he put his hand on the doorknob, it felt hot. He jerked his hand away.

He hurried to the window and looked out. Paul saw flames.

He coughed and fell to his knees. The air near the floor was clearer. He took a few deep gulps of air and stood up. He ran to a side window and saw more flames.

The arsonist had set his office on fire.

How was he going to get out of here?

He ran to the side door and wasn't surprised to feel the doorknob was also hot. He looked around, trying to find a way out. He wondered if he could get onto the roof and go over the flames, but there was no way onto the roof.

He ran back to the cell and grabbed the straw mattress off the metal frame. Back at the side door, he laid on the floor to catch his breath again. Then he stood up, pulled his shirt sleeve down over his hand, and opened the door.

He had to push hard because logs were leaning against it, which he expected. Flames rushed in, singeing him. He threw the mattress down, which momentarily created a clear path for him. He ran outside and a few yards from the building.

A crowd had already started forming a bucket brigade, but Paul could see it was too late. The fire had caught the roof on fire. The building would collapse soon.

He looked around and saw a familiar face in the crowd, someone who shouldn't be there. It was Abednego Long. Paul started toward him, but the collier disappeared into the crowd.

CHAPTER 7: READY FOR THE FIREFLIES

Paul Cresap had barely escaped being burned alive, but his office in the Mechanicstown Jail wasn't as lucky. The roof collapsed shortly after he made it out. He suspected he knew who had set the fire, and the charcoal he found around the building seemed to confirm it. It was most likely the work of a collier, and he had seen Abednego Hunt leaving the scene.

Paul would have followed him, but too many people wanted to know if he was all right and what had happened. It was dawn by the time he finally got his horse saddled and headed up to Abednego's camp on Catoctin Mountain.

Not unexpectedly, Paul found no one at the camp, but it was the only place he knew of where he might find. He had to check it first. As Paul rode around the camp looking for the collier, he spotted the handmade grave marker for Meshach Hunt, the brother Abednego had said fell into one of the charcoal stacks and died.

Paul saw no other sign Abednego might come back. Had he abandoned the camp entirely?

He rode his horse down to Catoctin Furnace to find the superintendent for the Catoctin Iron Works. The paymaster for the company directed Paul to a house outside of the village. The superintendent and his family would be staying there since an arsonist had burned the superintendent's house down yesterday.

"He's should still be out there," the paymaster said. "He hasn't been in today. He's probably trying to get things sorted out and order new furniture and clothing since he lost just about everything in the fire."

Paul thanked the paymaster and headed out to the house. It was about half the size of the ironmaster's mansion, but it was still much larger than the jail where Paul had been living for the past six months.

He knocked on the front door, but no one answered. He smelled smoke and saw a plume rising from the woods. The superintendent was probably there doing something. Paul walked into the woods and was surprised to see the gagged superintendent tied to a pole with a fire that had already been started under his feet.

Paul rushed forward and kicked at the logs, trying to disperse the fire and get it away from the man. He pulled off his vest and beat at the flames to keep them from spreading to the nearby brush.

Once the flames were out, he freed the superintendent and pulled the gag from his mouth. The man was singed a bit, but the flames hadn't caught his clothing on fire.

"What's going on?" Paul asked.

"It's Ben Hunt. He attacked me and did this."

"Where is he?"

"He was watching, but he ran deeper into the woods when he heard you coming."

"Why is he doing this?"

"I don't know. He's always been a loner and quiet, but he was a good worker," the superintendent said.

"What about his brother? Did his brother's death have anything to do with this?"

The superintendent's eyes narrowed. "Brother? Ben doesn't have a brother. He came in the other day wanting death benefits for his brother, but we don't have a record of a brother being employed by us."

"But his brother fell into the stack and burned to death. I saw the grave."

"I checked the records myself because Ben was so upset.

We have no brother or any other relative of his working for the company."

"Then what's he talking about?"

The superintendent shrugged. "I don't know. Ben works alone. It's the best situation. Colliers usually work in teams, in case someone falls through a stack. Ben wanted to work alone, and he does the same work per man as any of the teams, so we let him continue. He doesn't want to work with a team."

Paul walked the superintendent back to his house. Then he mounted up to ride back to the collier camp. If Ben Hunt didn't have a brother, who was buried in the grave?

Ben rode back to the collier camp. He wasn't sure why, perhaps it was because he had nowhere else to go. All Ben had wanted was his brother's death benefit from the superintendent, but the man wouldn't even admit Shack worked for him.

"Where have you been, Ben?"

Ben turned and saw his brother. Ben froze. "Shack? I saw you die."

Shack brushed non-existent dust off of himself. "I didn't. I got out of the stack, although I've got some burns. That's why I haven't been back. I collapsed in the woods and have been nursing myself back to health."

Ben ran over and hugged his brother. "Why didn't you let me help you?"

"You couldn't. You weren't ready."

"Ready? Of course, I was ready to help you. I tore the stack down looking for you."

Shack shook his head. "That's not what I mean. You weren't ready for the fireflies."

Shack threw his hand in the air and dozens of fireflies scattered in front of him, glowing like stars in the sky... or embers.

Paul rode into the collier camp and saw Abednego talking to himself next to a smoldering pile of charcoal, log fragments and dirt.

"Ben," he said.

The collier didn't seem to hear him. He was talking to someone Paul couldn't see. Ben walked to the stack he was near, still talking to no one Paul could see. Abednego didn't even notice that his shoe were smoldering.

"Ben, get out of the fire!" he called.

Ben didn't acknowledge him. He bent down and picked up a handful of charcoal embers. They were still smoking, but he acted as if nothing was wrong. He threw the embers into the air and they spread in a cloud around him.

Some of them fell on him, but he didn't react as if they were burning him. Some of them started catching his clothing on fire.

Paul ran over to him and pushed Abednego out of the fire. Then he got down next to him and rolled him over and over until the flames went out.

Once the flames were extinguished, he rolled Ben onto his stomach and tied his hands behind his back.

"I'm arresting you for arson," Paul said.

Ben still didn't seem to even know Paul was there.

Paul put the dazed man on the saddle and rode him back

to town. He carried him to Dr. Westgate to have his burns looked at.

"What's wrong with him?" Paul asked.

"You mean the burns?"

"No, he still doesn't seem to know we're here."

The doctor waved a hand in front of Abednego's face and snapped his fingers. Abednego didn't flinch or blink. "I noticed that. I think his mind might be broken. He should be in a lot of pain, but he doesn't seem to feel it."

"Why?"

"I don't know. It's beyond me. I could be the heat. It could be the solitude up on the mountain, or it might run in the family."

Paul rode back up to the collier camp. He walked over to the grave and started digging. If he could find a body, it would show whether Ben had a brother.

About a foot below the ground, he found a cigarbox. He opened it up and only found pieces of charcoal inside.

SET IN STONE

CHAPTER 1: MRS. ELIAS

The oldest male in each generation of Paul Carpenter's family had died suddenly. His father suffered a heart attack at age 45 and died the next day, but his two younger brothers were living healthy lives in their 70s. Paul's grandfather had been hit by a car crossing the street and died. His great-grandfather had been shot and killed fighting in Belleau Woods during World War I.

Paul wasn't sure why that thought occurred to him as he walked to his shop on North Church Street in Thurmont. It was a pleasant spring morning. He should be enjoying the warmth and thinking about his work for the day, but that maudlin thought had jumped into his mind.

Occupational hazard, he guessed. He was a stone carver, and most of the stones he carved were gravestones. So he was usually memorializing death at some point during his workday.

Then again, Paul's 55th birthday was approaching at the end of the month. He was older than most of the first-born men in his family had been when they had died. Paul wondered if he had escaped the family curse.

Curse? That's what his grandmother had called it. His father had never talked about it, and his grandmother had only explained it to Paul after his father had died. Paul had not believed it, as anyone would have. When he had asked his mother about it, she told him it was just a family superstition.

Curse or not, it would end with him. He had no son who would have to wonder if life would be inexplicably shortened.

Paul reached Carpenter's Memorials, a non-descript building that looked like it could have been a warehouse in a past life. The front yard was landscaped with shrubbery, flowers, and a fountain to hide the building's plainness.

He fished in his pocket for his keys, unlocked the door, and walked into the showroom. He noticed that the last person out the night before hadn't turned the lights off. He was going to have to post a notice reminding his employees to turn off the lights. Electricity was getting too expensive to be careless with it.

He walked into the break room and turned on the coffee-maker. Then he headed back to his office off the showroom to check his schedule for the day. He had a desk with a computer in it, but a large conference table dominated the room. He liked it because he could meet with clients at the table and spread out drawings of memorials. A set of bookshelves held binders with designs of different memorials, samples of fonts that could be engraved, and even samples of different types of stone. Pictures on the walls showed some of the most impressive monuments he had done, but he also liked to hang scenery shots he had taken during hikes on trails around the region. He found them peaceful. They allowed him to pull back from the intimacy of a gravestone and staring death in the face and know it was coming for you.

Paul checked his phone messages. He had only one call, but it was a hang up so he had nothing to worry about. His new e-mails were mostly junk, but he did see a few requests for bids he had submitted and an invoice for a shipment of marble.

He walked back to the breakroom for a cup of coffee and then came back to settle in for the morning. He pulled out his calculator, paper, and pencil and went to work coming up with a bid for what would be a pedestal for a bronze sculpture for a county park in Rockville.

Around 10 a.m., an older man entered the shop. He wore dark slacks and white socks and a yellow-striped shirt. He reminded Paul of a poorly dressed bumblebee. The man had a dazed look, which Paul was all too familiar with. It was grief.

"Good morning," Paul said. "May I help you?" Paul never smiled when he met someone in his business. Happy people rarely came to see him here.

The man looked around as if he was uncertain where the voice had come from. He finally focused on Paul and said, "My wife died last night."

"I'm sorry."

The man nodded.

"Why don't you come into my office and sit down?"

Paul showed him into the office and had him sit down at the conference table.

"Can I get you anything to drink?" Paul asked.

The man shook his head and stared at the table. Paul sat down across from him.

"How can I help you, Mr….?"

"Elias. Matthew Elias. I need a gravestone for Peg… Margaret… my wife."

Paul nodded. "I can help you, but are you sure you are in any shape to make decisions? It's only been a few hours since Peg died. You look like you are still in shock. Do you have a family member you can call?"

Matthew shook his head. "No. It was just me and Peg." He took a deep breath. "I can do this. I needed to get out of the house. I already talked to the funeral director."

"Do you have an idea what you want the marker to look like?"

"No, but I wrote down what it should say." He pulled a sheet of paper from his pocket and slid it across the table to Paul. He had written his wife's name, her birth and death dates, and "A wonderful woman."

"Well, let's start with having you look at the showroom.

You can see some popular designs and lettering."

They walked back out into the showroom and looked over the rows of blank gravestones sitting on the floor.

Paul said, "Take a look and see if there is something you like. If there isn't, that's fine, we can custom design something. However, if you can find something here that suits your needs, it will be less expensive."

Matthew started walking down the first row and looked at each stone. He touched a few, for some reason wondering how the stone felt. Matthew began to think that he would have to order something custom when he heard Matthew gasp.

"What is this?" Matthew nearly shouted.

Paul walked over to where Matthew was standing. He pointed at the stone in front of him.

"Why did you do this?" Matthew asked. "How could you know this?"

Paul looked at where he was pointing. The stone had been inscribed.

Margaret Elias
June 1, 1975—May 16, 2023
Beloved wife
She saw through him, and he took her eyes.

CHAPTER 2: MYSTERY MARKER

Paul Carpenter stared at the gravestone in his showroom that had already been engraved with the information for a dead woman, including an epitaph that read, "She saw through him and he took her eyes."

"Why would you do this?" Mark Elias, the dead woman's husband, had asked. He had come to Carpenter's Memorials inquiring about a gravestone for his wife. That had been the first time Paul had met Mark, and this was the first time he had seen this stone. It had been blank yesterday.

"I'm sorry, Mr. Elias. I can't explain this. You can see none of these stones have personal information on them," Paul said.

"Then how did it happen?" Mark asked, shaking a finger at the stone.

"I don't know. It was blank yesterday."

"Of course it was blank. My wife died overnight."

"That's what I mean. There was no one here who could have done that lettering. The shop was closed."

Mark pointed at the stone. "Well, someone did it."

Paul could understand Mark being upset. It must appear that Paul was trying to force him into buying the stone, but Mark had come here looking for a stone for his wife. He needed a grave marker. Why was he upset one was ready?

"Mr. Elias, I understand you are upset, but on my word, I did not do this. I didn't even know your wife was dead. I don't even know the two of you. That being said, this stone is of no use to me other than for display. If the information is correct, I can let you have it for half the cost."

"What? Why would I want this reminder in my wife's grave? You're lucky if I don't sue you!"

Mark Elias spun on his heels and stormed out of Carpenter's Memorials. Paul stared after him and then stared at the gravestone. Why was the man upset? He had come for a grave marker, and here was one. The engraving had been well done even if Paul hadn't been the one to do it. Paul had offered the man a bargain, so why had he acted as if it was an affront?

Then Paul read the epitaph again... it was odd.

He walked back into his office and flipped through the newspaper again. He didn't see any mention of Peg Elias, but her death might have happened after the newspaper's deadline. He got on his computer and opened his internet browser and typed in "Margaret Elias Thurmont, Maryland." As he scanned the hits that came up, he found one that looked like the right person.

It wasn't an obituary, though. It was a police report. Peg Elias had been murdered.

Paul read the article which said Peg had been last seen alive leaving Weis Market last night around 8 p.m. Security cameras showed her leaving the store. Police were alerted when patrons reported a filled shopping cart next to an empty car, which turned out to be her car. Around 2 a.m., an officer patrolling through Community Park found Peg's body propped up against a picnic table. No suspect had been identified yet, but it was less than a day since the murder.

Paul could understand why Mark was emotional, but it still didn't explain his reaction to Paul's offer.

When his employees came back after lunch, Paul gathered them in the showroom and pointed to the engraved stone.

"Does someone want to explain?" Paul asked.

"Do we need to load it on the truck for placement?" Joe Petrusku, his longest-serving employee, asked.

"No, because it hasn't been sold. In fact, Mr. Elias was in

here earlier looking for a stone for his wife. He saw this one and got very upset."

"Why? Is the spelling wrong?" Rick Smith asked.

"No, he hadn't ordered a stone," Paul said. "Who did this?"

"Don't look at me," Harley Peters said. "I don't know how to operate the engraving equipment."

"I didn't do it," Rick said.

"Me either. I don't even know Margaret Elias," Joe said.

Paul was inclined to believe them. They were all long-time employees who had shown themselves to be honest and hard working. Usually that would have brought Paul relief, but if none of his employees were responsible for this, who had come into his shop and engraved the blank stone? It would have taken more than one person to take the stone to the workshop where it could be engraved. It would have also been quite obvious that someone had been using the shop.

And the other nagging question was why would someone do this? It didn't make sense. Someone had to know Margaret had been killed, snuck in here, and engraved the stone. It would have taken hours and more than one person to move the stone to the engraver and back. It was Georgia granite and weighed over 300 pounds.

Paul worried over the problem all day. The only anomaly he could see was that whoever engraved the stone had left the lights on. He checked with his employees, and they all denied leaving the lights in the showroom on.

Paul even called the police to report what had happened. They took his report, but didn't seem too concerned.

However, near the end of the day, a Thurmont Police detective showed up and asked to see the engraved stone. He asked if anyone had touched the stone. Paul thought about it, and said, "Not today, but I can't say for certain about yesterday or before."

Detective Weissman dusted the stone for fingerprints. He took three sets of prints off the stone. He also took Paul's fingerprints and the employees' to eliminate them.

"So, is this related to Mrs. Elias's murder?" Paul asked.

Detective Weissman rubbed his chin. "Yes, but I'm not sure how or why."

"Do you know why Mark Elias reacted so badly to this?"

"Other than seeing his wife's name on a gravestone?"

"Well, I can understand being upset. I've seen that happen even when people order a stone marker, but he wasn't sad or despondent about this. He was angry."

The detective looked at the stone and back at Paul.

"You know Mrs. Elias was murdered," the detective said.

Paul nodded. "I looked it up on the Internet after her husband left, trying to figure out why he was mad."

"He didn't tell you?"

"No, he only said she had died."

"One of the things we left out of the press release was that whoever killed Mrs. Elias also took her eyes."

CHAPTER 3: VERONICA TRESSELT

Although it seemed a waste to have security cameras throughout Carpenter Memorials, their presence brought some relief to Paul Carpenter. He still did not know how someone had apparently entered his business and engraved a blank grave marker with the information of a woman who had died hours earlier, let alone why.

Paul did his best to put the unusual occurrence behind him, but just when that seemed to happen, he walked into the showroom one morning to find the lights on again. He paused. That had been the first sign that something had been wrong two weeks ago, although he hadn't realized it at the time.

He stepped into the showroom and said, "Hello!"

No answer. He hadn't expected one. He was always the first person to work. He walked along the rows of display headstones, looking for one that was out of place. He saw Peg Elias's stone and shook his head. He couldn't sell the stone, and so it remained as a memorial to something unexplained that had happened here.

In the next row, he found the Georgia granite monument with brand new engraving on it.

Veronica Tresselt
April 2, 1940 – May 30, 2023
He took her heart. He took her life.

Knowing what had happened with Peg Elias, he doubted Veronica Tresselt had died pleasantly.

Who was doing this? If it was the murderer, why was he doing it? What purpose did it serve? If it was someone else, why didn't the person take his information to the police?

Paul walked back to the workshop where the engraving machine was located. He saw no stone dust or sand on the floor and no used stencil in the trash.

That gave Paul an idea. He went back to his office and turned his computer on. He searched for files on Margaret

Elias and Veronica Tresselt. If someone had used the engraving machine, they would have needed to enter the information that would be needed to guide the sandblaster. The last job Paul saw entered was one he had done three days ago for John Brighton.

The work couldn't have been done by hand. Even using the engraver, it would have taken all night. Lettering the stone by hand would have taken a couple days of steady work. It would have been noticed.

"This isn't funny anymore," Paul muttered. Not that it had been funny to start with.

Someone was trying to make some sort of statement, not that Paul knew what he was trying to say. It was costing Paul a lot of expensive stone, though.

He pulled up his Internet browser and typed in "Veronica Tresselt." He got hits on the name. He could tell she lived in Thurmont, but he saw nothing to indicate she had died. It could be like it had been with Margaret. She had been killed overnight. Her name probably wouldn't show in the obituaries until tomorrow.

Worse, since she was probably killed, her name would start showing up in the news later this morning.

Paul waited all day, wondering if someone would walk into the shop looking for a grave marker for Veronica Tresselt. He even avoided leaving for lunch because he didn't want to miss someone who might come in.

He checked the news sites regularly and found no reference to Veronica.

Maybe she wasn't dead. Maybe this was some elaborate hoax. He found a phone number for Veronica online, but when he called it, no one answered, and no answering machine picked up.

Paul went out to the showroom and looked at the newly engraved headstone for what must have been the twentieth time today. Why would someone go to so much trouble to be so cruel to someone? And why had they chosen to do this in Paul's showroom?

Something moved in the corner of his eye. He looked at the hallway leading back to the workroom. The lights were off so he only saw dark shadows. However, those shadows seemed to move.

He walked toward the hall, not sure what he expected to see, but all he saw was darkness. He shook his head and went back into his office. He was getting paranoid.

The next day, he saw a story about Veronica Tresselt in the newspaper. It was an obituary, which was a relief. He had expected to see another murder story as he had with Peg Elias. It was just a standard obituary. It didn't say how Veronica had died, only that she had been a widow who had been found dead in her home after a welfare check.

He called up his security camera video and started scrolling back to the night when the grave marker had been engraved. He should have thought to look at this yesterday, but he had been worried about finding out if Veronica had been murdered.

The cameras were set up to send him a notice if the cameras picked up anything. He hadn't received any notices. The only thing Paul had seen so far was only himself as he entered and left the business when he turned the camera system on or off.

As he watched the footage from two nights ago, he saw the lights come on in the showroom, but he didn't see anyone walking through the showroom.

He looked at Veronica's stone because he knew something had to happen to it. The lights stayed on, and Paul had a good view of the front of the stone. Then in the midst of the lighted showroom, a dark shadow fell across the marker that was so dark, Paul couldn't even see the marker. He didn't see anything that could be causing it, and nothing else seemed to be cast in shadows.

After a minute, the shadow faded. Then the letters started appearing on the stone as if someone was writing the information. The letters were engraved as if someone was using his finger to write in sand. Sandblasting would have taken much longer to wear away the granite. It continued until the lettering was complete. Then nothing else. The headstone was fully engraved.

Paul sat forward in his chair.

What had just happened?

CHAPTER 4: THE VIEWING

Paul Carpenter wasn't sure why he had decided to attend Veronica Tresselt's funeral. Maybe he felt some responsibility for her death because someone who had been involved with it had engraved her headstone in his shop. Of course, he didn't know who that person was or how it had been done without leaving any evidence of it happening other than the headstone. Maybe he was here to find answers. Either way, he found himself standing outside of Stauffer Funeral Home on East Main in Thurmont.

He took a deep breath and walked inside. He knew many of the staff from having worked with them over the years on various funerals. He nodded his head at them and looked for the viewing room where Veronica would be.

"What brings you here, Paul?"

Paul turned and saw Heather Carmichael, one of the funeral directors, standing next to him.

"I came for Veronica Tresselt's viewing," he said.

"Was she a friend?"

"No. Just someone I knew in passing, but I wanted to pay my respects."

Heather shook her head. "Terrible what happened to her. Two horrible murders in Thurmont in a month. What's this place coming to?"

"I wish I knew because I wish it would end."

Two murders. Peg Elias was the first. Her husband had come to Carpenter's Memorials for a headstone for his murdered wife and found one already engraved, although none of Paul's employees had done the work. Then yesterday Paul had found another engraved stone. This one had Veronica's information on it, although luckily none of her family had visited the shop and gotten a surprise at seeing a finished stone like Mark Elias had.

He walked into the viewing room. It was about a third full. He had been hoping more people would be here already, so he wouldn't have to engage in small talk.

He ignored the heads that had turned in his direction and headed to the front of the room where casket sat on the draped bier with the lid open.

He took a deep breath and stepped up next to the casket. Veronica Tresselt was an old woman who had been 82 years old when she was killed. She looked kindly, but then, kindly people are just as likely to be killed as cantankerous ones. Her white hair was styled and her makeup carefully applied. She wore a pink dress with lace cuffs.

Paul stared at her chest, looking for some tell-tale sign that her heart had been removed. He wasn't sure what to expect. A depression over where her heart had been? The funeral home had done a good job preparing the body. He would recognize good work when he saw it even if he wasn't a mortician.

He was a fourth generation stone carver. The Carpenters had arrived from Ireland shortly before the beginning of the Civil War and made a good living as undertakers throughout the war. That was the first time an oldest son died before his time. Neil Carpenter had been killed at the Battle of Antietam, leaving behind a young wife and infant son. Following the war, the family moved into creating markers and monuments. That is when they learned stone carving. It was a fortuitous move since states and military companies wanted monuments erected in memory of their fallen citizens and comrades.

Paul's mother had always said something happened to make family get into the undertaking business. Paul had thought it was the war, but he discovered years ago that they had come to the United States before the war started. The war just started them on the road to success.

Paul realized he had been staring at Veronica too long, and he stepped back. He didn't even know that her heart had been taken, but that is what the epitaph on the mysteriously engraved stone had said. "He took her heart. He took her life."

Peg Elias had had a similar mysterious epitaph on her stone that read, "She saw through him, and he took her eyes." And according to the police, whoever had killed her had taken her eyes.

"I'm sorry," Paul whispered. "If I knew what was going on, I would have helped."

And he would have if he knew what was going on and why his shop was connected to these murders.

Paul turned to go. He started walking toward the exit from the room when he saw Detective Weissman standing at the back of the room staring at him. Paul walked into the hallway where Weissman met him.

"I'm surprised to see you here, Mr. Carpenter," the detective said.

"I had another blank stones get carved yesterday."

"Why didn't you call me?"

"I didn't know until today that it had been this lady. No one from her family came to see me."

Weissman nodded. "And you still don't know how this person is doing it?"

Paul shook his head. He was reluctant to tell the detective about the video surveillance since he didn't understand what he had seen.

"So why did you come here?" Weissman asked.

"Did… did she have her heart taken or was she stabbed or shot in the heart?" Paul asked.

Weissman's eyes widened slightly. He hesitated and then

finally nodded. "Her heart was taken. It was something we left out of the press releases. How did you know?"

"The epitaph."

"That again."

"Don't you have any leads on who did it? This is freaking me out."

"I wish I could say we knew how your business was connected, but we are still investigating."

CHAPTER 5: A CHANCE

Jennifer Pendergast
August 10, 1950 –
In the hours before death she knew peace.

When Paul Carpenter read the inscription on the grave marker he knew had been blank the night before, he kicked the stone. Then, because the stone was hundreds of pounds of granite, he yelled in pain.

It had happened again. He had suspected as much when he found the lights of the showroom on when he arrived. Somehow, someone had managed to engrave a grave marker and clean up after themselves, leaving no trace they had broken into Carpenter's Memorials other than a freshly engraved marker.

As Paul hopped around because of the pain in his toes, he realized this grave marker was different than the other two. He looked at it again. It didn't have a death date.

Was this woman not dead yet?

The epitapth had referred to her death.

Paul shook he head. He considered going to engraving room, but he knew he wouldn't find anything. He had found no evidence of the engraving machine was used, and if the video evidence was to be believed, he wouldn't find anything.

He walked into his office and called up the video from last night. It was the same thing that had happened the night that Veronica Tresselt had died. The lights in the showroom came on, seemingly by themselves. A shadow appeared and moved across the stone, hiding it from sight. Then the shadow faded and the letters started appearing on the stone as if someone was writing in the sand.

Despite the engraving being done right in the showroom, Paul saw no evidence of it. There was no sand or grit on the floor from the letters. What had happened to the stone that had been removed from the engraving? Had it just disappeared?

Paul wasn't sure why he was surprised. Nothing about what had happened with these apparently self-engraving headstones made any sense to him.

So why hadn't this woman's death date been filled in?

He searched the Internet for Jennifer Pendergast, but he didn't find anything about her. None of the hits that came up on his search were for a local woman, and he didn't find any obituaries.

Paul gave up and called Detective Weissman at the Thurmont Police Department. He was the detective Paul had told about the other two incidents with grave markers. The detective came out later that afternoon, and Paul showed him the video and the carved stone.

"What is going on here?" the detective asked, pointing at

the video.

"I have no idea. I've only seen this once before with Veronica Tresselt's stone. The video showed the same thing."

"Can I have someone look at this footage?"

Paul nodded. "I can e-mail the file to you, but what about the woman?"

"We haven't heard anything about the death of anyone named Jennifer Pendergast, and I haven't heard of any Jane Does either."

Paul tapped the computer screen. "There's no death date on this stone. Maybe she's still alive. Can you find her?"

"Maybe." The detective didn't sound all that certain.

Detective Wiessman returned to the shop the next day.

"We found Jennifer Pendergast," he said.

"Is she okay?" Paul asked anxiously. For once, he didn't want to hear that someone had died. It wasn't a matter of him looking for business. Someone's life was at stake.

"No. She was murdered last night."

Paul hurried out to the showroom and looked at the stone with Jennifer Pendergast's name on it. The death date was still blank. He had half-expected to find it filled in, although he hadn't seen any signs of a mysterious nighttime visitor.

Detective Weissman followed him into the showroom. "What's the matter?"

"I wanted to see if the death date had been filled in."

"Did you expect it to be?"

Paul shrugged. "I don't know. I have no idea how this is happening or why."

"The thing is, Jennifer Pendergast's death looked natural,

143

but because of what is happening here with the stones, we looked closer. That's how we discovered it was a homicide. This one wasn't brutal like the other two."

"Another murder."

"Do you know who could be doing this?"

Paul shook his head. "I can't even tell you how it's being done. You saw what I saw on the security video."

"The epitaph," the detective said. "I wonder why."

"You and me both."

"Well, because these stones connect all three murders, we think we might have a serial killer on our hands."

CHAPTER 6: THE FAE

Paul Carpenter unlocked the door to Carpenter's Memorials and saw that the showroom light was already on. He shuddered because he knew what it meant. Three times already he had come to work and found the lights on, and each time, he also found a grave marker engraved for someone he didn't know.

He walked through the showroom, looking at the markers for Margaret Elias, Veronica Tresselt, and Jennifer Pendergast. They mocked him and his inability to make sense of what had happened. Then he saw the new one that had been engraved:

Paul Carpenter
June 12, 1967 – June 12, 1923
The firstborn is the first to die.

Paul woke up in a cold sweat. He sat up in his bed and

looked around. He'd had another bad dream. They were becoming more frequent the longer the serial killer went uncaught.

He poured himself coffee and toasted a bagel. Then he decided it was time to get a new perspective on things. His dream had connected his family "curse" of the firstborn sons dying unnatural deaths with the serial killer of three women in Thurmont.

Paul called his mother. She lived in the Lutheran Retirement Village in Gettysburg as a widow. She had never remarried after his father had died.

She answered the phone on the second ring, and they shared the typical pleasantries they spoke of whenever he called. Then he finally got to the point of the call.

"Mom," Paul said. "I've been wondering lately about the family curse. I want to know more about it." He heard only silence. "Mom?"

"It's not a curse. It's bad luck," she said finally.

"What can you tell me about it? When did it start? Is there a reason it started?"

"I don't know anything about it, Paul. Your father never thought much about it. The few times it came up when the family was together, he always shrugged it off. Don't you worry about it, Paul. It's just bad luck."

"There's been some weird things happening at work the past couple months. It made me think about the curse. I just thought it might be connected somehow. I need answers. I've been having bad dreams about this."

More silence, then, "Maybe you should call your grandmother. She's the only person I heard call it a curse. Get her to tell you why."

Unlike his grandfather, Paul's grandmother was still alive and doing well at 99 years old. She was even looking forward to turning 100 in a few months.

When Paul finished speaking with his mother, he decided to call his grandmother. She was happy to hear from him, but less so when he explained why he called.

"It's nothing you can do anything about, Paulie," she said. "If it is going to happen to you, it will happen."

"I'm just trying to figure out why my nightmares connected them. Please, tell me what you know. Maybe it will help. Maybe it won't. I have to try."

He heard his grandmother sigh. "You have to understand that the family doesn't talk about it much. I think some of them are afraid that if they do, what happens to the firstborn will happen to them.

"It worried your grandfather something fierce, though. He always made sure to have plenty of life insurance, even when we couldn't afford it.

"I don't think anyone really knows why it happens, but there's a family legend. The way your grandfather explained it to me was that before the Civil War, his great-grandfather captured a fae in Ireland."

"Wait. Fae? Isn't that a fairy?"

"Yes."

Paul wondered if his grandmother was losing it.

"Aren't they supposed to be harmless?"

"Maybe if they existed, but this is a family legend. Anyway, your great-great-great-grandfather somehow captured this fae and planned on putting it on display to make money. However, the fae bargained with him, and they worked out an exchange. Your great-great-great grandfather agreed to release the fae if he made him wealthy.

"The agreement was struck, but somehow in the language of the agreement, the fae managed to get itself allowed to take the firstborn son of the firstborn sons when it wanted. It bound to the Carpenter bloodline."

This was making less and less sense.

"Why would anyone make such an agreement?" Paul asked.

"I don't know. The fae tricked your great-great-great grandfather or maybe he was too blinded by the idea of finally having money that he didn't notice. Most of all, like I said, this is a family legend."

"But the family has been well off since we came to America," Paul said.

"And you think a fae has something to do with that? More likely, it's hard work and a decent business sense of our family."

Paul finished the conversation with his grandmother and went into work. Luckily, the lights weren't on. He was surprised at how tense he became nowadays whenever he came to work.

Would the lights be on or off? It have never meant anything to him before, other than his employees had been careless. Now, it meant the difference between someone having been murdered or not.

The day was uneventful, except that when Paul was closing things up for the night, he noticed a shadow moving on the hallway to the workshop. Nothing was back there that should have been moving, and it reminded him of the other shadow he had seen in the hall weeks earlier. That shadow had moved by itself, too.

"Who's there?" he called out. There was no response, and without thinking, he blurted out, "Are you the fae?"

To his surprise, a small man about two feet tall walked into the showroom. Despite his height, he was proportioned as an adult male. Paul blinked in surprise, but was too shocked to say anything.

"Been doing a little research, have you?" the small man said. He wore a small black suit with a green vest and a bowler hat.

"Who are you?"

"Now, I won't be givin' you my name, lad. That's part of the reason I'm in this predicament in the first place. Names give a person power over the named."

"Are you really the fae that has been killing my family?"

The little man snorted. "I'm the one who has been making your family rich."

"By killing them."

The fae tilted his head to the side. "How else am I to uphold my bargain? We fae live long lives, but not long enough to manage your finances. I must be around to maintain your wealth because your family doesn't seem to have much business sense. But to stay alive, I take the life energy of just one person from each generation."

Paul pinched his hand just to make sure he wasn't having another nightmare. He didn't wake up.

"How do I make this stop?" Paul asked. "How do I break the contract?"

"Give me my freedom."

"No one is holding you prisoner. I didn't even know about you until today."

The fae stomped his foot on the floor. "The magic enforces the contract. It's the way of my people."

"So why let me see you?"

The fae chuckled. "I know the old lady told you about me, sort of, at least what she knew. You will give me my freedom, though. It's not up to you, anymore."

"How?"

"I can only take the life of the firstborn after the firstborn son is born. The contract magic protects your life until then. You haven't married yet, so it is doubtful there will be another born. So when you die, I can't get your life energy, and so, you will break the contract. I'll be free to return to my homeland."

"So why are you inscribing the murder victim names on the grave markers. How does that help you?"

The fae held up a tiny finger. "For one, it's fun. I can frustrate everyone." He held up a second finger. "I find that knowing the end of the contract is near makes me excited to rush it along. I can't take direct action against you to help you die. The contract protects you. I can let the killer believe you know who he is."

"I don't."

The fae smiled. "That's the beauty of it. It doesn't matter.

He believes and will come for you, and since no one knows who he is, you can't stop him. Maybe I'll engrave a new headstone one day just for you. I'll leave the death date off so you can wonder, but I'll write on it: *Paul Carpenter. Money isn't everything.*"

CHAPTER 7: ENDING THE CONTRACT

Since his encounter with a fae, Paul Carpenter had found himself tense and paranoid. The little creature had told him that his engraving of the headstones for victims of a serial killer had been done on purpose to send the killer to Paul. Paul's death would free the fae from his contract with Paul's family.

So, Paul knew a killer would be coming for him. He just didn't know when.

The waiting, the not knowing was wearing him down. Every person who approached him was a potential killer. He was even starting to think people he knew might be the killer.

And every morning, Paul checked the markers in the showroom, expecting to see a new one engraved with his information.

He was trying to concentrate on work one morning when the doorbell rang, noting that the front door had opened. Paul stiffened with dread and then forced himself to relax.

He stood up and straightened his shirt. Then he walked out into the showroom. A man in his late twenties or early thirties was standing there, looking a bit confused.

"Hello, may I help you?" Paul asked.

"Yes, I need a grave marker for my mother. She died yesterday, and I need to make the funeral arrangements."

"I can certainly help you with that Mr...."

"Smith. Bob Smith."

Paul brought Bob into his office where they discussed the options, the budget, and what Bob wanted the marker to say. Then they walked out into the showroom to look at the different marker designs.

"Why are some of them engraved?" Bob asked.

"Sometimes families order markers and then for some reason, they never give us a delivery site." It was a lie, but it sounded reasonable to Paul. "If the design is still available, we continue to use it as a display piece."

"It makes this room sort of look like a graveyard."

Paul looked around. He had never thought of it that way, but he could see how someone might think that.

Paul felt a sharp pain in his side and yelled. He looked down and saw that Bob had stabbed him with a knife.

Bob grabbed him with his free hand. "How did you know?"

This was the killer! He had finally come for Paul.

He fell back against one of the grave markers. It was the one for Veronica Tresselt.

"How did you know?"

"From the markers."

"But how did you know what to put on the markers? I can't let you tell the police anymore. I already have to move because of you."

He raised the knife to stab at Paul again. Paul felt his

hand on one of the stone vases that they offered as an option. He grabbed it and swung it at Bob. It hit him on the side of head and knocked him away.

Paul knew he needed to get to a hospital. He could feel the wetness of blood inside of his shirt and pants.

Bob came at him again and Paul swung the vase, hitting Bob's hand and knocking the knife from it. But Paul lost his grip on the vase and it fell to the floor.

"Help!" Paul yelled, hoping his employees didn't have machinery on in the workroom. "Help!"

Bob looked around to see if someone was coming. Paul punched him. Bob staggered and tripped on the vase on the floor. He fell backwards and hit his head on the back of the stone that had been engraved for Margaret Elias. Then he lay still.

Joe Petrusku came hurrying in from the back. "Did you yell?"

"Get the police and an ambulance!" Paul yelled as he sagged against a grave marker. He pinched at the flesh around his stab wound and hoped it hadn't hit anything vital.

He looked over at Bob. He couldn't tell whether the man was dead or unconscious, but at least he wasn't coming at Paul.

"At least I know I fight better than an old lady," Paul murmured.

The ambulance arrived and the EMTs did what they could to stop the bleeding. Then they loaded him into the ambulance and took him to Frederick Memorial Hospital. The doctors stitched him up and told him he would recover, but they wanted to keep in the hospital overnight for observation.

Detective Weissman and another police officer arrived early in the morning as Paul was eating as passable breakfast.

"The man who attacked you was Brian Stockman. Do you know him?" the detective asked.

Paul shook his head. "He said his name was Bob Smith."

"So you told the police yesterday."

"Did you check him out? I think he is the killer."

Weissman nodded. "We got a search warrant for his apartment. We found trophies of his kills."

"Trophies?"

"Mrs. Elias' cameo necklace. Mrs. Tresselt's glasses, and one of Mrs. Pendergast's shoes. We can connect him to all three murders."

Paul sighed. "I'm glad you caught him."

"I also found something odd when I went back into your shop today."

"What?"

"Another grave marker was engraved."

Paul groaned. "Another victim?"

Detective Weissman shook his head. "Almost. This one had your name on it, and an epitaph that read: Next time. Do you know what it means?"

Paul shook his head. "I thought those engravings would end since you caught him."

The detective shrugged. "Maybe they will, but let me know if another shows up."

When Paul walked into his house later that day, he sat in his favorite armchair and relaxed. It was over. He could feel the weight of those women's deaths off his shoulders.

But he knew it wasn't done. The fae would just try something else. He had been thinking about it all day.

"Let me live!" Paul called out. "If you trying something else, I will change my will to have me cryogenically frozen when I die."

He watched shadows shift around his living room and he heard a chuckle. Then the room darkened. When it lightened, Paul saw the fae standing in front of him. He was a perfectly formed two-foot-tall man wearing a black suit, green vest, and bowler hat.

"That wouldn't help," the fae said.

"Really?"

"You'd still be dead."

"Would I? I would have a chance of being revived, so doesn't that mean I wouldn't be quite dead. There's a possibility I could come back. I bet your agreement with my great-great-great-grandfather didn't take into account something like that. What would that do to your contract? Would it be in force again? Would it not be broken until I was dead and buried?"

The fae's eyes narrowed as he glared at Paul. "I don't know."

"Then you had better leave me alone, or you might create a big problem for yourself."

The fae grumbled, but he faded into the shadows.

That wasn't the end of Paul's plan, though. It was only a way to gain him some time to put the rest of the plan into place.

Two years later, Paul married. It was to a woman he had

been been dating, once he allowed himself to get out more and not be so focused on his work. The following year, he and his wife, Morgan, adopted a young boy from Russia.

When the final papers were signed and Noah was officially his son, Paul finally breathed a sigh of relief. Although Paul now had a son to continue his family, he wasn't of the Carpenter bloodline so the fae could not take Paul's life.

The contract would end, but not until Paul died his natural death.

Bon Appetit

Chapter 1: The Guests

Stephen Carter stood in the doorway to Culinare´ waiting for the people who held his future in their hands. In the past, they had loved him; they had hated him. He had always sought their love, while seething silently at their scorn. But tonight... tonight he sought a different objective. Not love or hate, but memory. Whatever else happened tonight, they would remember him.

He watched the vehicles arrive one by one at the restaurant that was located between Emmitsburg and Thurmont, not far off US15 in a renovated 1880s farmhouse. He had added rooms to the house, a patio, a curved drive, and everything else the Frederick County Planning Commission had required. The cars stopped in front of the restaurant to discharge their passengers. This was just another one of the many dinner parties Master Chef Carter had thrown over the years to introduce his new dishes to food critics.

He had closed up Culinare´ for the night so that the dinner would be a private party between him and his critics, where Stephen could control all elements that might affect their opinions to the fullest. Closing down the restaurant would probably cost him about $3,000 for the night, but it was necessary. Critics could sometimes be very vocal about their feelings, which could be very upsetting to paying patrons. Besides, critics are all prima donnas at heart, and a private meal is like a private viewing to a film critic. Satisfied egos keep stomachs settled even if the dish might not agree with their cultured taste buds.

Besides, with good reviews, Stephen could recoup his lost sales in a matter of days with increased business from people who read the reviews. With this in mind, he had prepared what he considered more than those Burger King critics deserved. He considered this meal his ultimate creation, and he planned to do everything he could to get those pretty words flowing from their keyboards when they reviewed his meal.

Bradley Tarson arrived first, smoking a disgusting cigar.

This only proved Stephen's point about critics being tasteless. He felt no one whose mouth was constantly assaulted by tobacco could appreciate the flavor of a fine meal. However, Bradley wrote for *The Washington Post* Food Section, so Stephen smiled and tried not to cough when Bradley blew a cloud of smoke around his face.

Jessica Harrison arrived next. Perhaps of all the critics attending, she was the one Stephen appreciated most. Not because she loved his food; quite to the contrary, she detested it. Jessica's saving grace was that she was herself a delicious dish, and the night of this dinner party was no exception. She wore a lovely red evening gown that hugged every curve of her body.

Next, Lawrence Grant. To say he was a pompous ass was to give him a compliment. He believed that any entree priced under $100 was fast food. His reviews in *Cuisine* were nothing more than physical descriptions of the food's appearance. He had been known to give bad reviews simply because a few grains of rice had spilled onto the steak when the plate was placed on his table.

The only person missing was Mitchell Reed. If his words were knives, then Stephen would be chopped and diced by now. Mitchell hadn't been able to make the dinner, but Stephen was sure the critic would be here in spirit. He certainly wouldn't miss a chance to denounce Stephen's delectable entrees as a waste of whatever animal had given its life for the meal.

Most people would think that Stephen was foolish for inviting his worst critics to the party. Stephen saw it differently. He needed this group's approval only because to date they hadn't approved of any of his entrees. Cooking was Stephen's life. He had been doing it for longer than he had been married, and he loved it more than he loved his wife Gloria.

As usual, Stephen sat at the head of the table since he was the host. He used a large rectangular table laid out with fine linen, which he only used on special occasions. The glasses were hand-cut crystal, the dishes were bone china, and the silver was engraved sterling.

Everyone looked uncomfortable at first, even a little more quiet than usual. Stephen was sure they had noticed that none of them had ever given him a great review, and they were surprised at how small the dinner party was. Needless to say, they weren't sure how to act until they saw the dinner, then their claws came out.

Wayne, the head waiter, brought out the artichokes with olives a la Grecque and set them before everyone, particularly careful to give Lawrence the most-perfect salad Stephen could prepare. He had carefully measured out portions and matched colors of vegetables. Otherwise, the appetizer was nothing fancy. Just a small warm up for the main course. The critics dove in with glee, except for Lawrence. He took notes on the appearance of the salad before he even touched his fork to the bowl, but even his astute observations could not guess what Stephen had substituted for anchovy fillets.

"Smells a bit foul, don't you think?" Jessica asked as she picked at the greens with her fork. "It clashes with my perfume."

Bradley laughed and downed a glass of sherry. He smiled

J. R. RADA

and poured himself another glass. "Well, even if the meal flops Stephen, I'll still say you have great taste in wine. What will we be having with dinner?"

"Chianti. From Fabre´, an old Italian vineyard," Stephen answered.

Bradley nodded his approval.

Stephen tasted his own salad happy with the flavor of the marinade; it was flavored with his own secret ingredient, which served to complement the entree. Jessica winced slightly at her first taste of it. Stephen thought for a moment he had already lost points with her, but then she smiled.

He almost laughed. If only she knew.

"This is delicious, Stephen." She smiled with her full, red lips. "If your new entree is as good, I may actually have to break a tradition and give you a good review."

Ah, the words Stephen longed to hear!

Bradley agreed. "You do seem to have risen above average with this marinade, Stephen. What's in it?"

"Let's just say it's a secret ingredient for now. It's made especially to complement the rest of the meal. I feel each element of a meal is like part of a body. The appetizer is the brain, the salad the skin, the entree the heart, the dessert the stomach, and the wine the blood. They all work together to create one entity, in this case, the meal."

"You've become a philosopher," Bradley said. He held up his glass of sherry. "Oh, but if I were a blood brother to a grape."

Everyone laughed. What's a party without a sot—or as Bradley would call himself, a connoisseur.

160

"Too bad Mitchell's not here. He might even have liked this," Lawrence said as he finally finished taking notes and began eating.

"He was invited, but he wasn't able to come this evening," Stephen told the group.

"What a shame," Jessica said shaking her head. "You could have made him eat his words after that scathing review he gave you last week."

Stephen sighed and shrugged his shoulders. "Perhaps, I deserved the review he gave me."

"What?" Lawrence said, quickly scribbling down Stephen's quote in his notebook. "I've never known you to say that you deserved a poor review. I remember the venison dish you prepared last year." He frowned as he recalled it. "When I told you it tasted like tar, you broke my glasses and pencil."

Stephen flinched, remembering that review. It had taken his business weeks to recover from that little experiment with new meats. It would have been a success, too, if Mitchell's review hadn't caused Stephen to put aside his other ideas.

"Well, in Mitchell's case, I was distracted. My wife and I had been having some problems. We still are. Lots of arguing and threats being bandied about. The night Mitchell came to the restaurant had been after a particularly bad fight. I was too upset to concentrate on my work. I think I might have mismeasured some of the ingredients." Stephen tried to look ashamed. "Not very professional I admit, but I'm only human."

"I agree with Jessica. This meal may redeem you,"

Bradley said.

Everyone seemed in such a good mood, Stephen decided to capitalize on their good spirits. He signalled Wayne to bring out the entree. He set a steaming plate in front of everyone. Underneath the creamy red sauce, the meat chunks were a rich brown. Beneath the meat was Stephen's own mixture of seasoned wild rice. Lawrence immediately started scribbling. Bradley sniffed the plate as if it were a wine, and Jessica poked at the meat under the sauce.

"What do you call it?" Jessica asked.

"I haven't decided yet. Maybe you can help me decide on a name after you've eaten," Stephen offered.

CHAPTER 2: THE MEAL

The three food critics looked at the exquisite meal that that Stephen Carter had placed before them. It was his ultimate creation, and his grand attempt to get united praise from the critics who had worked so hard to tarnish his life's work to create the most delicious meals ever crafted. Only Mitchell Reed was missing.

Bradley Tarson speared a small piece of meat, smelled it, and chewed it slowly. After he swallowed, he smiled broadly. "Excellent. What gives it such a rich flavor?"

"It's natural flavoring. The spices only serve to bring it out more fully."

"Do you cook like this at home, Stephen?" Jessica Harrison asked.

Stephen shook his head. "Gloria doesn't like to be around when I'm cooking. It makes her nervous. I don't blame her either. Sometimes I look at those knives and think how easily they would slice through her flesh."

The critics suddenly looked at each other uneasily. Lawrence looked at his meat a little more closely.

"I had a wife once," Bradley said, breaking the tension. "A shrew to say the least. Always tossing my cigars in the garbage disposal. She used to constantly yell at me, 'You're smoking cancer sticks!' or 'Don't critique my food unless you want to eat off the floor!'"

This was a fascinating bit of self-revelation on Bradley's part. Stephen had trouble believing he had anything in common with the critic beyond food. "Did you critique her food?" Stephen asked.

Bradley nodded and smiled. "Definitely. And if you think I give your dishes a hard time, I had to invent a substandard rating system for Phyllis' meals."

"Did she make you eat your food off the floor?" Lawrence Grant asked.

"She tried."

"What did you do?"

"Why I divorced her. Irreconcilable differences. I was a gourmet, and she was a glutton."

Everyone laughed.

"I would have dished her up and served her for dinner," Stephen announced.

That shut everyone up. Lawrence swallowed the piece of meat he was eating as the smile fell from his face. Jessica pushed her plate away, gulped down the last of her chianti, and quickly refilled the glass.

"Stephen, I am truly curious now. The meat has such a

unique flavor and the sauce, too. What is it?"

The master chef shook his head. "It's a special dish I created just for tonight. I've wondered all my life how to prepare it properly, and I finally figured it out a week ago. Who knows? If it goes over well with you three, I may make it a permanent menu item."

"It has to be something uncommon," Jessica guessed. "I've tasted most types of beef, poultry, and fish. Have you started experimenting with game again? Is it venison?"

Stephen shook his head. *Wrong.*

"Bear."

Another shake. *Wrong again.*

"Alligator," Bradley said, taking his best guess.

Three strikes. You're out.

"No, Bradley. Just enjoy it."

"How can I enjoy it? I don't know what it is."

Stephen just smiled. The cat that swallowed the canary (but of course, the entree wasn't fowl, either).

Lawrence put his hand on his stomach. "I'm not sure if I'm hungry any longer."

Stephen frowned at him. "What does hunger have to do with it? This is business. I made this meal especially for all of you. I figure if I can please my worst critics with it, then I can please anyone. You're not afraid to give me a good review are you?"

"Certainly not." Lawrence cut a piece of meat and chewed on it. It no longer looked enjoyable to him, though.

These people should know better than anyone how just the right words could turn a person's stomach.

"Now have you ever thought about how much meat you

could get from a person? Someone like the Rock would give you a lot of thick steaks, but would probably be tough meat. Now my wife, on the other hand, would be tender meat; as tender as this entree. Of course, she has no breast meat, if you know what I mean," Stephen said as his critics ate.

Dangle the bait and see if they take it. Stephen thought he could have been a professional fisherman as well as a master chef.

Jessica brought her napkin to her mouth. Was there a lady-like way to vomit? Stephen wondered if he was about to find out.

"I find all this cannibalistic talk quite distasteful at dinner," she said.

Ah, yes, hook, line, and sinker.

Stephen heard the front door slam closed. Only a few people had a key to Culinare´, and only one would ever slam the door. Everyone knew he hated that, and only one person couldn't have cared less.

His wife Gloria stormed into the dining room, heels clicking on the hardwood floors and jewels dangling around her neck. "Well, isn't this sweet? Just a bunch of friends, Stevie, or is business that bad since Mitchell's review?" she said putting her hands on her hips and striking an indignant pose.

Her appearance was a bit ill-timed perhaps. Stephen had so wanted to torture the dinner guests through until dessert.

He stood up. "Gloria, these are my critics. Critics, this is my wife, Gloria."

Stephen heard an audible sigh of relief from them.

"Just peachy," Gloria announced in a voice he had once

found arousing. "What I want to know, Stevie, is why my credit card got rejected?"

Stevie. Only she would call him that because she knew it sounded like chalk scratching a chalkboard to Stephen's ear.

"Simple. I had it canceled," he told her.

"You what?"

"A credit card is not a magic wand that pays for things with fairy dust, although you seem to think it is. However, when your card balance went into five digits, the magic went out of it."

"But how will I buy things?" No more arrogance in her voice.

"You won't," Stephen explained.

"But that's not fair." Gloria could whine better than a distraught child.

"Oh, it's quite fair. And if you don't want me to make you start returning some of the things you've already bought, you'd better go home. We'll discuss it later."

Gloria fumed and he knew she wanted to say something, but Stephen could see her taking inventory of her jewelry and wardrobe and wondering what she would be left with. She had no doubt her husband would be true to his word if she argued. So she turned and left the same way she came in... loudly.

Stephen sat back down and apologized to his guests. No one seemed to mind. Jessica smiled again. Bradley suddenly laughed.

"What's so funny, Bradley?" Stephen asked.

He looked mildly embarrassed but said, "You had me worried for a minute or two, Stephen. All this talk about a secret meat and how you wanted to cut up your wife. I was beginning to wonder if you hadn't done her in and were using us to get rid of the evidence."

Stephen laughed.

"It's not funny. I thought so, too. And I was especially worried since I actually liked the dish," Jessica added.

"You do? That's wonderful." The chef turned to Lawrence. "What about you? Did your careful observations tell you you were eating my wife's rump roast?"

He shrugged. "I couldn't tell, and I consider myself the expert. I'm happy you're just being mysterious and not murderous because I do like it," he said as he ate another mouthful.

In fact they had all started eating again. "I take it I'll get favorable reviews all around on this new entree." Three nods. A first... at least from them. Stephen wondered if Mitchell would have liked it.

"Delightful. Then I feel I have achieved what I set out to do," Stephen said.

"What's that?" Lawrence asked, always curious.

"How to stop you three from being food critics."

CHAPTER 3: JUST DESSERTS

The three food critics sitting alone at a table in Culinare´ looked at one another and then at Master Chef Stephen Carter who owned the upscale restaurant between Thurmont and Emmitsburg. No one knew quite what to say. Stephen had invited them to an exclusive meal, supposedly with the hopes of getting a good review, but Stephen had just told them he was going to stop them from being food critics.

"I don't understand," Jessica Harrison said. "Is that a bad joke that you'll stop us from being critics by getting a good review?"

They had all loved Stephen's specially prepared meal. He had never taken such care to cook and present a more perfect meal. And his hard work had paid off. He had won them over. They had eaten the meal and drunk his wine and complimented him on the meal.

Stephen smiled. "No, I will stop you by making the job quite distasteful for you. You are all petty power mongers who know nothing about creating a meal, especially Mitchell. I only wish he could have been here." Mitchell Reed was the only critic of Stephen's four worst critics who wasn't at the table.

"You certainly don't know how to handle a compliment," Bradley Tarson said, swilling down his third glass of Chianti.

"By the way, you haven't been eating my new entree. This is my new dessert," Stephen announced proudly.

"Don't be foolish. This is meat," Lawrence Grant said.

Stephen shook his head. "I am the chef, and I decide what it is. This is my new dessert. I call it Just Desserts."

Lawrence stood up and threw his napkin on his plate. "I've had enough of this. I'm going home. If you thought I gave you a hard time before Stephen, wait until you see what I write tomorrow."

Stephen glanced at his watch and then shook his head as he crossed his arms over his chest. "I don't think so. Don't tell me such esteemed food critics as yourselves can't identify my mystery meat?"

"We already told you we can't," Jessica said. "I've never tasted anything like it before. That's why I was afraid it might be Gloria."

"You set us up, didn't you?" Bradley said. "All that talk about cutting your wife and breast meat. You wanted us to think we were eating your wife so you could get your petty revenge."

Bradley might be a bit tipsy, but he wasn't stupid. However, he was wrong.

Stephen shook his head and smiled. "It wasn't that at all. I talked about Gloria because I didn't want you to know you were eating Mitchell Reed."

The critics gasped and grabbed for their glasses of wine while Stephen laughed.

"You're crazy!" Bradley yelled.

Stephen stood up. "I am not. I am defending my creation, my love, from being destroyed by you."

"Someone call the police," Jessica said.

Stephen glanced at his watch unconcerned. Lawrence started to dial his phone and fell flat on his face. Bradley walked over to him.

"I should be the one falling over drunk, you fool. Can't you do anything?" Bradley said.

Instead, Stephen answered, "He's dead, Bradley. None of you bothered to ask about the sauce."

"What about..." Jessica started to say, but her eyes rolled back in her head and she fell onto the table, dead.

"Not quick enough, my dear," Stephen said.

"You poisoned us," Bradley said just before he died.

"I call it my meat tenderizer." Stephen turned his head

169

over his shoulder. "Wayne!"

Wayne stuck his head through the door. "Yes, boss?"

"Here's tomorrow night's special. You'd better marinade them."

In the end, the critics gave Stephen a good review of his new dish, and he loved them; everybody *loved* them.

CONFESSIONS

CHAPTER 1: NIGHTMARES

Cal Winter stood under the shower head, letting the warm water wash over his face and down his body. Something tapped his ankle, and he kicked it away with his foot. He tilted his head back so the water could gently massage his throat. Again, something bumped into his ankle. This time from the other side.

Thinking it was the bar of Ivory soap floating around in

the tub, Cal reached down for the soap.

Instead, he grabbed someone's arm.

He opened his eyes and saw that he was standing under the shower head, but instead of standing in water, he stood in a pool of blood. The bar of Ivory soap was nowhere in sight. What he did see was a dismembered body. Hacked off arms, legs, feet, hands floating in the bloody water.

Cal threw the arm away from him. Then from the bottom of the tub a woman's head bobbed to the surface. It was Diane's face. Her gray eyes had rolled back in their sockets so that Cal could only see the white undersides, and it was that blind stare that made him scream.

He woke up in his bed, the scream dying on his lip. He wiped his sweaty face on the sheets and turned on the bedside lamp.

Everything was fine. He was in his bed in his bedroom in his apartment above East Main Street in Thurmont.

He climbed out his bed and walked out of his bedroom to the bathroom. Hesitating at the door, he took a deep breath and turned on the light.

No blood. No body parts.

He walked to the tub and looked inside. It looked as it should. The only discoloration was the brown ring about midway up the side of the tub. That was because he hated cleaning his apartment.

Cal sighed and went back to bed. It had just been a bad dream. Nothing to worry about. It was just the greasy enchilada he had eaten for dinner making itself known. He should have gone to Los Amigos. The food was better, but he couldn't afford to eat out lately.

Why had he dreamed about his ex-wife? He hadn't seen her for six months since they walked out of the courtroom in Frederick after the divorce was finalized. By then, he had already moved his things into this apartment and whatever wouldn't fit he had sold. He had left Diane with as little as he could since she was getting more of his paycheck than him nowadays. He hated the woman, and many times, he had wished her dead but certainly not the way he had seen her in his dream. His stomach trembled at the thought.

Cal couldn't bring himself to go back to sleep. He laid in bed for the rest of the night until his alarm rang at six o'clock. He staggered out of his bed to the bathroom. He usually took a morning shower to wake himself up, but the dream from the night before was still too fresh in his mind. Instead of the shower, he filled the sink with water and soaped himself up. He was surprised when he saw red scratches on his arms. He didn't know how they had gotten there. He couldn't remember getting scratched recently.

He was also surprised at how exhausted he felt. His dreams must have disrupted his sleep enough that he didn't get any rest.

Fifteen minutes later, he was dressed and making his breakfast in the kitchen. He read the morning news on his phone while he ate his breakfast.

Cal almost choked on a sausage link. The lead story on the Frederick News Post website was of a dead woman whose dismembered body had been found in her tub in a pool of bloody water. She had been murdered sometime around six or seven o'clock the night before. Her body had been discovered around midnight when her roommate came home from a date.

Gina Lamarck.

Cal didn't recognize the name or the face in the black-and-white photo that the paper had printed. It hadn't been the face he dreamed of seeing in the tub. Gina Lamarck didn't resemble Diane in the slightest. Gina was younger, a brunette, and slightly overweight. Diane was forty, a bleached blond, and very fit from her all of her aerobics classes.

Yet he had dreamed about Gina's death.

His stomach twisted in a knot. He dropped his phone and ran into the bathroom where he quickly gave back the breakfast he had just eaten. Standing on shaking legs, he washed his face off.

"It's just a coincidence," he whispered to his reflection in the mirror above the sink.

His reflection didn't look like it believed him.

Almost a week went by between Cal Winter's first and second nightmares where he dreamed of murders and dead bodies.

The first nightmare was when he saw Gina Lamarck's death. He didn't know her, but he had seen her dismembered body in his nightmare. The sight lurked among his waking thoughts. How had he dreamed of the murder? He had followed Gina Lamarck's murder investigation in the news, hoping to find some clue that would give him a reason that he had dreamed about Gina's murder. He had even ventured so far as to call Diane and see if she knew Gina Lamarck. It hadn't been a pleasant conversation.

Cal should have been able to guess how the conversation

would go when a man, obviously Diane's latest conquest, answered the phone.

"May I speak with Diane Winter?" Cal had asked.

"I think you have the wrong number," the man said sleepily.

"Is this 555-1809?"

"Yea, but there's no Diane Winter here."

"How about Diane Stanislav?" Cal asked, using his ex-wife's maiden name.

"Oh, yea. Wait a minute. Diane! Someone's on the phone for you, babe!" the man called out.

From somewhere in the distance, Cal heard someone say, "Who is it?"

"I don't know, but he thought you were Diane Winter."

"Hello," Diane said.

"Diane, this is Cal."

The tone in her voice changed instantly. She should have kept the name Winter. It fit her attitude perfectly, at least where Cal was concerned. "Oh, I should have known. I told everyone that mattered that I was using my maiden name."

As if she could remember being a maiden, Cal thought, but wisely didn't voice.

"Diane, I'll make this as short as possible. I don't really want to be talking to you either, but I need to know something. Do you know anyone named Gina Lamarck?"

"No, why did you hook yourself up with some loser?" she asked.

"Are you sure you don't know her?"

"Yes, I'm sure."

Cal hung up.

It gave him a slight pleasure to be able to leave his ex-wife hanging like that. Let her wonder what was going on. Why should he know? He certainly didn't.

Why had he connected Diane with Gina Lamarck's murder? Then remembering the conversation, he thought maybe he had heard about the murder on the late news and thought it was a shame someone hadn't done the same thing to Diane.

CHAPTER 2: FISHING

Gina Lamarck was the first dead woman Cal Winter dreamed about, although he didn't know who she was. He only discovered that later from reading the news.

Unfortunately, she wasn't the only murdered woman he dreamed about.

In his second nightmare, he was in his kitchen cooking dinner. He had been fishing at the Frank Bentz Pond west of town and brought home two trout to fry. He wrapped one of the fish up to freeze for another meal. The second fish he held over the sink and scaled. Then he cut the tail and head off and slit the belly so he could debone the trout.

As he opened the filets, he screamed. Staring back at him from inside the trout was a gray eye. Cal picked up the filleting knife he had dropped and slowly reached out to prod the eyeball with the point of the knife. It rolled to the side of the fish.

Cal picked up the cutting board and swept the fish and the eyeball into the garbage can. However, the eyeball missed the trash and fell onto his foot.

Cal screamed again and woke up.

He lay in his bed trying to catch his breath. He knew he had only been dreaming, but it had seemed so real. He could smell the fish and feel the weight of the eyeball as it fell on his foot. Were dreams that realistic? His hand shook as he wiped the cool sweat from his face.

Why was he having these horrible dreams?

He woke up more tired than usual. He thought that besides scaring him, the nightmares must also be troubling his sleep. He *knew* they were troubling his sleep.

In the morning, he read about the murder of Holly Nash. Her body had been found in Big Hunting Creek. Forensic pathologists estimated she had been dead for a day. The cause of death was strangulation. The body was intact except that one of Miss Nash's green eyes was missing. The police assumed that fish had eaten it because there were signs that they had also begun to eat other parts of her body.

Cal pushed his cereal bowl away. He wasn't sure if he would ever eat again. He stomach felt so upset.

Was he a psychic? Was that why he was having these dreams?

He didn't want to have them, though. They scared him with the richness of the macabre details.

He'd never shown a tendency to be psychic before. He couldn't even read Mark deMauer's poker face at their weekly poker games.

Besides weren't psychics supposed to be more specific about what they saw? Cal had no idea what his dreams meant until he saw the news reports. Holly Nash had green eyes. The eye he had dreamed seeing had been gray, the color of

Diane's eyes.

At least he hadn't dreamed the dead woman was Diane, though he was furious with her. He had gotten a credit-card bill yesterday for $9,000, and he hadn't made any of the charges. Then he had realized Diane must still have a credit card in his name and was using it.

He had called Diane. This time she had answered.

"I got the bill for all of your charges. I hope you're going to pay for it," Cal said.

Diane laughed. "The credit card is not in my name. Diane Winter made those charges on Cal Winter's card. I'm Diane Stanislav." She had laughed again and hung up on him.

Cal had screamed and banged the phone against the table so hard that the earpiece broke off. It was when she made him this mad that he wished she was dead.

Cal began to go to bed each night scared. What terror would wake him? Whose murder would he see? Not having a nightmare was almost as bad as having one. The suspense of not knowing when the next nightmare would come raised the stress he felt. He had to do something or he would have a breakdown. He had to stop the nightmares, and to do that, he had to stop the murders.

Cal walked into the Thurmont Police Station, nervously twirling his hat in his hands. He had called the police station an hour ago to talk to whoever was in charge of Nash and Lamarck murders. The Thurmont Police were only handling the Lamarck murder. The Frederick County Sheriff's Office was in charge of the Nash murder.

He was transferred to the Detective Wycoff's extension.

When Cal told the detective he might have some useful information about the two cases, Detective Wycoff had asked Cal to come down to the station.

"I'm here to see Detective Wycoff," Cal told the woman behind the window at the front desk.

She motioned Cal to a side door and opened it for him. The police officer pointed to a black man seated behind a desk in the middle of the open room.

"That's him."

Cal walked over to the desk and Detective Wycoff looked up from his paperwork. "Mr. Winter?"

"Yes, sir."

Wycoff smiled. "You don't have to call me, sir. Detective will do. Have a seat and tell me about this information you have."

Cal sat down and looked around at the other officers in the room. They all seemed to be staring at him. "The two women who were murdered—Gina Lamarck and Holly Nash—well, I sort of dreamed about their murders before they happened or maybe while they happened."

The detective looked skeptical. "What do you mean *sort of?*"

The detective poured Cal a cup of coffee as Cal explained his dreams. He left out the fact that the face he had seen in the tub hadn't been Gina Lamarck's but his ex-wife's. He only thought it would make him sound crazier if the detective knew he had dreamed about killing his wife.

"Are you a psychic, Mr. Winter?" Detective Wycoff asked when he had finished.

Cal shook his head. "No, that's why it's so surprising.

That, plus the weird images of the nightmares. I want the nightmares to stop. They are affecting my sleep so that I always feel tired, though I sleep through the night." Cal paused. "You don't believe me, do you?"

The detective shrugged. "It doesn't matter if I do or not. Other than the fact that you've connected the murders, you're not seeing anything but the aftermath. You aren't able to tell us where to find the bodies or who does the killing or even who the next victim is going to be. That doesn't help much."

"Oh." Cal was disappointed that he couldn't be more help.

"What about a motive? Why would this person want to kill these women?" Detective Wycoff asked.

"I don't know. I don't dream about them before the murder, only what I see afterwards, just like you said."

"Listen, if you have another one of those dreams, call me. Maybe it will be more helpful."

CHAPTER 3: CONFESSION

Cal Winter slept only a few hours each night, and each of those hours were troubled. His lack of sleep was beginning to make him irritable. He was so scared he felt as if he were about to lose his sanity.

Four nights after his visit to the Thurmont Police, Cal had another dream. He was walking down an unfamiliar street at night. He heard a clock chiming the time and he looked up to see what time it was. The clock was on top of an old warehouse and was backlit so the numbers could be easily read.

It was one o'clock in the morning. Cal wondered why he should be out at that time of night. Then he remembered he wasn't outside. He was dreaming. He was seeing through the killer's eyes like in the other dreams.

As Cal stared at the hands of the clock, he realized something was wrong with them. He tried to focus on them and realized that real hands had been speared on the ends of the clock hands.

Cal woke up.

It was three o'clock in the morning.

He called Detective Wycoff the next morning and asked him if the police had found a pair of hands mounted on the hands of clock.

"Did you have another dream, Mr. Winter?" the detective asked.

"Yes, and I know that the murder happened sometime before one o'clock."

"How do you know that?"

"When I dreamed I saw the hands, it was one o'clock in the morning."

"Frederick Police found the hands, and the body was inside the warehouse."

"Was it another woman?"

"You don't know?" Detective Wycoff sounded tense, even irritated.

"I only saw the hands from a distance."

"Her name was Jennifer Mason. She was killed in the warehouse loft, and the killer cut off her hands with a hatchet. Then the killer used the clock access panel on the loft to reach outside and place Ms. Mason's hands on the clock hands." The detective paused. "Thank you for your information, Mr. Winter. I'll keep what you told me in mind."

Cal finally reached a point where he tried to stay awake constantly. Why should he even attempt sleep if it would only show him a nightmare? Yet no amount of coffee or activity could keep him awake. Even as he felt himself falling asleep, he began to cry.

He dreamed again. This nightmare was just as odd as the others, but at the same time different. Cal was staring at a group dangerous-looking people around him. They were dressed like prisoners. They shouted things he didn't understand. One man punched him. Then Cal felt a pain in his side. He looked down and saw a piece of metal in his side.

When he woke up, his side throbbed. He took a shower and wondered if he should call the police. Even if the detective believed him, what could Cal tell him that might help? He hadn't seen a murder this time.

Cal went into the kitchen and poured himself a cup of coffee and sat down to read the morning news. He didn't see mention of any odd murders and he was beginning to think last night's nightmare had just been a normal nightmare. It seemed almost a relief compared to the others.

Someone knocked at his door. When Cal answered it, it was Detective Wycoff and a Frederick County Sheriff's Deputy.

"Did you find something out about the murders, Detective?" Cal asked as he let them in.

"Yes, we have, Mr. Winter." The police officers sat down on the sofa across from Cal. "Why did you get divorced, Mr. Winter?"

Cal wondered what that had to do with anything. "My wife was cheating on me."

"Your wife told us it was because you abused her, and she thought you might even kill her."

Cal started to rise out of the armchair he was sitting in. "That's a lie!"

Detective Wycoff pulled out his handcuffs and quickly snapped them over Cal's wrists.

"What are you doing?" Cal asked trying to jerk his hands away.

"We're arresting you for the murders of Gina Lamarck, Holly Nash, and Jennifer Mason," Wycoff said.

"But I didn't do anything. I only dreamed about them."

The detective shook his head. "I don't know what your scam is unless you were trying to taunt us or see how the investigation was going," he said angrily.

"But I tried to help you."

Detective Wycoff poked his finger in Cal's chest. "We found your fingerprints on the clock and in Gina Lamarck's bathroom. We might not have been able to trace them, except you made yourself a suspect by coming to me and knowing too many details. I had your fingerprints lifted from the coffee cup you used when you were down the station. It matched the ones we found at both the Lamarck and Mason murders. And since you connected all three murders, we can assume you also committed the Nash murder, too. We'll find the proof. Your wife gave us enough information to establish your history of violent behavior. Who were the women, Mr. Winter? Dates? Or just randomly chosen women you saw on the street?"

Cal's face turned red with anger. "But I didn't do anything but try to help you! My wife was lying to you. I never laid a hand on her."

"The doctor and the judge thought differently. It was even recommended you seek psychiatric help. Did you?"

"I'm not crazy!" Cal screamed.

"I hope you're not. We've got enough to send you to send you to prison for life."

Cal remembered his last nightmare, and realized it probably wouldn't be spending a long time in jail. Life sentences only lasted a lifetime. He wouldn't be too long.

ABOUT THE AUTHOR

J. R. Rada is the Amazon.com bestselling author of *Kachina, The Man Who Killed Edgar Allan Poe,* and *Welcome to Peaceful Journey.*

He works as a freelance writer in Gettysburg, Pennsylvania, where he also lives with his wife and sons. James has received many awards from the Maryland-Delaware-DC Press Association, Associated Press, Maryland State Teachers Association and Community Newspapers Holdings, Inc. for his newspaper writing.

To see J. R. Rada's other books, visit his website (jamesrada.com/jrrada).

If you would like to be kept up to date on when J. R. Rada's new books are published or ask him questions, you can e-mail him at *jimrada@yahoo.com.*

PLEASE LEAVE A REVIEW

If you enjoyed this book, please help other readers find it. Reviews help the author get more exposure for his books. Please take a few minutes to review this book at Amazon.com or Goodreads.com.

If you enjoyed *Shades & Shadows*, keep up to date on new releases, news, and specials from J. R. Rada by joining his mail list. When you sign-up at https://bit.ly/3CILHI6, you'll get *Polderbeest* as a FREE gift.

Made in the USA
Middletown, DE
22 September 2024

61039247R00106